MEMORIES

MEMORIES:

A STORY OF GERMAN LOVE

BY

MAX MÜLLER.

TRANSLATED FROM THE GERMAN
OF

GEORGE P. UPTON.

Fredonia Books
Amsterdam, The Netherlands

Memories:
A Story of German Love

by
Max Müller

ISBN: 1-4101-0420-6

Reprinted from the 1900 edition

Fredonia Books
Amsterdam, The Netherlands
http://www.fredoniabooks.com

In order to make original editions of historical works available to scholars at an economical price, this facsimile of the original edition of 1900 is reproduced from the best available copy and has been digitally enhanced to improve legibility, but the text remains unaltered to retain historical authenticity.

CONTENTS.

TRANSLATOR'S PREFACE

TRANSLATOR'S PREFACE.

THE translation of any work is at best a
difficult task, and must inevitably be pre-
judicial to whatever of beauty the original pos-
sesses. When the principal charm of the original
lies in its elegant simplicity, as in the case of the
"Deutsche Liebe," the difficulty is still further
enhanced. The translator has sought to repro-
duce the simple German in equally simple English, even at the risk of transferring German
idioms into the English text.

The story speaks for itself. Without plot,
incidents or situations, it is nevertheless dramat-
ically constructed, unflagging in interest, abound-
ing in beauty, grace and pathos, and filled with
the tenderest feeling of sympathy, which will go
straight to the heart of every lover of the ideal

in the world of humanity, and every worshipper
in the world of nature. Its brief essays upon
theology, literature and social habits, contained
in the dialogues between the hero and the heroine, will commend themselves to the thoughtful
reader by their clearness and beauty of state-
ment, as well as by their freedom from prejudice.
"Deutsche Liebe" is a poem in prose, whose
setting is all the more beautiful and tender, in
that it is freed from the bondage of metre, and
has been the unacknowledged source of many
a poet's most striking utterances.

As such, the translator gives it to the public,
confident that it will find ready acceptance
among those who cherish the ideal, and a tender
welcome by every lover of humanity.

The translator desires to make acknowledg-
ments to J. J. Lalor, Esq., late of the Chicago
Tribune, for his hearty co-operation in the pro-
gress of the work, and many valuable sugges-
tions; to Prof. Feuling, the eminent philologist,
of the University of Wisconsin, for his literal

version of the extracts from the " Deutsche The-
ologie," which preserve the quaintness of the
original, and to Mrs. F. M. Brown, for her
metrical version of Goethe's almost untrans-
latable lines, " Ueber allen Gipfeln, ist Ruh,"
which form the key-note of the beautiful harmony in the character of the heroine.

G. P. U.

Chicago, November, 1874.

AUTHOR'S PREFACE

AUTHOR'S PREFACE.

WHO has not, at some period of his life, seated himself at a writing-table, where, only a short time before, another sat, who now rests in the grave? Who has not opened the drawers, which for long years have hidden the secrets of a heart now buried in the holy peace of the church-yard? Here lie the letters which were so precious to him, the beloved one; here the pictures, ribbons, and books with marks on every leaf. Who can now read and interpret them? Who can gather again the withered and scattered leaves of this rose, and vivify them with fresh perfume? The flames, in which the Greeks enveloped the bodies of the departed for the purpose of destruction; the flames, into which the ancients cast everything once dearest

to the living, are now the securest repository
for these relics. With trembling fear the sur-
viving friend reads the leaves no eye has ever
seen, save those now so firmly closed, and if,
after a glance, too hasty even to read them, he
is convinced these letters and leaves contain
nothing which men deem important, he throws
them quickly upon the glowing coals — a flash
and they are gone.

From such flames the following leaves have
been saved. They were at first intended only
for the friends of the deceased, yet they have
found friends even among strangers, and, since
it is so to be, may wander anew in distant lands.
Gladly would the compiler have furnished more,
but the leaves are too much scattered and muti-
lated to be rearranged and given complete.

FIRST MEMORY

FIRST MEMORY.

C HILDHOOD has its secrets and its mys-
teries; but who can tell or who can explain
them! We have all roamed through this silent
wonder-wood — we have all once opened our eyes
in blissful astonishment, as the beautiful reality
of life overflowed our souls. We knew not where,
or who, we were — the whole world was ours and
we were the whole world's. That was an infinite
life — without beginning and without end, without rest and without pain. In the heart, it
was as clear as the spring heavens, fresh as the
violet's perfume — hushed and holy as a Sabbath
morning.

What disturbs this God's-peace of the child?
How can this unconscious and innocent existence ever cease? What dissipates the rapture of

this individuality and universality, and suddenly leaves us solitary and alone in a clouded life?

Say not, with serious face, it is sin! Can even a child sin? Say rather, we know not, and must only resign ourselves to it.

Is it sin, which makes the bud a blossom, and the blossom fruit, and the fruit dust?

Is it sin, which makes the worm a chrysalis, and the chrysalis a butterfly, and the butterfly dust?

And is it sin, which makes the child a man, and the man a gray-haired man, and the gray-haired man dust? And what is dust?

Say rather, we know not, and must only resign ourselves to it.

Yet it is so beautiful, recalling the spring-time of life, to look back and remember one's self. Yes, even in the sultry summer, in the melancholy autumn and in the cold winter of life, there is here and there a spring day, and the heart says: "I feel like spring." Such a day is this — and so I lay me down upon the soft moss of the fragrant woods, and stretch out my weary limbs, and look up, through the green foliage, into the boundless blue, and think how it used to be in that childhood.

Then, all seems forgotten. The first pages of memory are like the old family Bible. The first leaves are wholly faded and somewhat soiled with handling.. But, when we turn further, and come to the chapters where Adam and Eve were banished from Paradise, then, all begins to grow clear and legible. Now if we could only find the title-page with the imprint and date — but that is irrevocably lost, and, in their place, we find only the clear transcript — our baptismal certificate — bearing witness when we were born, the names of our parents and godparents, and that we were not issued *sine loco et anno.*

But, oh this beginning! Would there were none, since, with the beginning, all thought and memories alike cease. When we thus dream back into childhood, and from childhood into infinity, this bad beginning continually flies fur-

ther away. The thoughts pursue it and never
overtake it; just as a child seeks the spot where
the blue sky touches the earth, and runs and
runs, while the sky always runs before it, yet still
touches the earth — but the child grows weary
and never reaches the spot.

But even since we were once there — wherever
it may be, where we had a beginning, what do
we know now? For memory shakes itself like
the spaniel, just come out of the waves, while
the water runs in his eyes and he looks very
strangely.

I believe I can even yet remember when I
saw the stars for the first time. They may have
seen me often before, but one evening it seemed
as if it were cold. Although I lay in my mother's
lap, I shivered and was chilly, or I was fright-
ened. In short, something came over me which
reminded me of my little Ego in no ordinary
manner. Then my mother showed me the
bright stars, and I wondered at them, and
thought that she had made them very beauti-

fully. Then I felt warm again, and could sleep well.

Furthermore, I remember how I once lay in the grass and everything about me tossed and nodded, hummed and buzzed. Then there came a great swarm of little, myriad-footed, winged creatures, which lit upon my forehead and eyes and said, "Good day." Immediately my eyes smarted, and I cried to my mother, and she said: "Poor little one, how the gnats have stung him!" I could not open my eyes or see the blue sky any longer, but my mother had a bunch of fresh violets in her hand, and it seemed as if a dark-blue, fresh, spicy perfume were wafted through my senses. Even now, whenever I see the first violets, I remember this, and it seems to me that I must close my eyes so that the old dark-blue heaven of that day may again rise over my soul.

Still further do I remember, how, at another time, a new world disclosed itself to me — more beautiful than the star-world or the violet perfume. It was on an Easter morning, and my mother had dressed me early. Before the window stood our old church. It was not beautiful, but still it had a lofty roof and tower, and on the tower a golden cross, and it appeared very much older and grayer than the other buildings. I wondered who lived in it, and once I looked in through the iron-grated door. It was entirely empty, cold and dismal. There was not even one soul in the whole building, and after that I always shuddered when I passed the door. But on this Easter morning, it had rained early, and when the sun came out in full splendor, the old church with the gray sloping roof, the high windows and the tower with the golden cross glistened with a wondrous shimmer. All at once the light which streamed through the lofty windows began to move and glisten. It was so intensely bright that one could have looked within, and as I closed my eyes the light entered my soul and therein everything seemed to shed brilliancy and perfume, to sing and to ring. It seemed to me a new life had commenced in myself and that I was another being, and when I asked my mother what it meant, she replied it was an Easter song they were singing in the church. What bright, holy song it was, which at that time surged through my soul, I have never been able to discover. It must have been an old church hymn, like those which many a time stirred the rugged soul of our Luther. I never heard it again, but many a time even now when I hear an adagio of Beethoven's, or a psalm of Marcellus, or a chorus of Händel's, or a simple song in the Scotch Highlands or the Tyrol, it seems to me as if the lofty church windows again glistened and the organ-tones once more surged through my soul, and a new world revealed itself — more beautiful than the starry heavens and the violet perfume.

These things I remember in my earliest childhood, and intermingled with them are my dear mother's looks, the calm, earnest gaze of my father, gardens and vine leaves, and soft green

turf, and a very old and quaint picture-book—
and this is all I can recall of the first scattered
leaves of my childhood.

Afterwards it grows brighter and clearer.
Names and faces appear—not only father and
mother, but brothers and sisters, friends and
teachers, and a multitude of *strange people*. Ah!
yes, of these *strange people* there is so much re-
corded in memory.

SECOND MEMORY

SECOND MEMORY.

NOT far from our house, and opposite the old church with the golden cross, stood a large building, even larger than the church, and having many towers. They looked exceedingly gray and old and had no golden cross, but stone eagles tipped the summits and a great white and blue banner fluttered from the highest tower, directly over the lofty doorway at the top of the steps, where, on either side, two mounted soldiers stood sentinels. The building had many windows, and behind the windows you could distinguish red silk curtains with golden tassels. Old lindens encircled the grounds, which, in summer, overshadowed the gray masonry with their green leaves and bestrewed the turf with their fragrant white blossoms. I had often looked in there, and at evening when the lindens exhaled their per-

fumes and the windows were illuminated, I saw
many figures pass and repass like shadows. Music swept down from on high, and carriages drove
up, from which ladies and gentlemen alighted
and ascended the stairs. They all looked so
beautiful and good! The gentlemen had stars
upon their breasts, and the ladies wore fresh
flowers in their hair; and I often thought,—
Why do I not go there too?

One day my father took me by the hand and
said: "We are going to the castle; but you must
be very polite if the Princess speaks to you, and
kiss her hand."

I was about six years of age and as delighted
as only one can be at six years of age. I had
already indulged in many quiet fancies about the
shadows which I had seen evenings through the
lighted windows, and had heard many good
things at home of the beneficence of the Prince
and Princess; how gracious they were; how much
help and consolation they brought to the poor
and sick; and that they had been chosen by the

grace of God to protect the good and punish
the bad. I had long pictured to myself what
transpired in the castle, so that the Prince and
Princess were already old acquaintances whom
I knew as well as my nut-crackers and leaden
soldiers.

My heart beat quickly as I ascended the high
stairs with my father, and just as he was telling
me I must call the Princess "Highness," and the
Prince "Serene Highness," the folding-door
opened and I saw before me a tall figure with
brilliantly piercing eyes. She seemed to advance
and stretch out her hand to me. There was an
expression on her countenance which I had long
known, and a heavenly smile played about her
cheeks. I could restrain myself no longer, and
while my father stood at the door bowing very
low — I knew not why — my heart sprang into
my throat. I ran to the beautiful lady, threw my
arms round her neck and kissed her as I would
my mother. The beautiful, majestic lady willingly submitted, stroked my hair and smiled;

but my father took my hand, led me away, and
said I was very rude, and that he should never
take me there again. I grew utterly bewildered.
The blood mounted to my cheeks, for I felt that
my father had been unjust to me. I looked at
the Princess as if she ought to shield me, but
upon her face was only an expression of mild
earnestness. Then I looked round upon the
ladies and gentlemen assembled in the room,
believing that they would come to my defense.
But as I looked, I saw that they were laughing.
Then the tears sprang into my eyes, and out of
the door, down the stairs, and past the lindens in
the castle yard, I rushed home, where I threw
myself into my mother's arms and sobbed and
wept.

"What has happened to you?" said she.

"Oh! mother!" I cried; "I was at the
Princess', and she was such a good and beautiful
woman, just like you, dear mother, that I had to
throw my arms round her neck and kiss her."

"Ah!" said my mother; "you should not

have done that, for they are strangers and high dignitaries."

"And what then are strangers?" said I. "May I not love all people who look upon me with affectionate and friendly eyes?"

"You can love them, my son," replied my mother, "but you should not show it."

"Is it then something wrong for me to love people?" said I. "Why cannot I show it?"

"Well, perhaps you are right," said she, "but you must do as your father says, and when you are older you will understand why you cannot embrace every woman who regards you with affectionate and friendly eyes."

That was a sad day. Father came home, agreed I had been very uncivil. At night my mother put me to bed, and I prayed, but I could not sleep, and kept wondering what these strange people were, whom one must not love.

———

Thou poor human heart! So soon in the spring are thy leaves broken and the feathers

3

torn from the wings! When the spring-red of
life opens the hidden calyx of the soul, it per-
fumes our whole being with love. We learn to
stand and to walk, to speak and to read, but no
one teaches us love. It is inherent in us like
life, they say, and is the very deepest foundation
of our existence. As the heavenly bodies incline to and attract each other, and will always
cling together by the everlasting law of gravita-
tion, so heavenly souls incline to and attract
each other, and will always cling together by the
everlasting law of love. A flower cannot blossom without sunshine, and man cannot live without love. Would not the child's heart break in
despair when the first cold storm of the world
sweeps over it, if the warm sunlight of love from
the eyes of mother and father did not shine
upon him like the soft reflection of divine light
and love? The ardent yearning, which then
awakes in the child, is the purest and deepest
love. It is the love which embraces the whole
world, which shines resplendent wherever the

eyes of men beam upon it, which exults wherever it hears the human voice. It is the old,
immeasurable love, a deep well which no plum-
met has ever sounded; a fountain of perennial
richness. Whoever knows it also knows that in
love there is no More and no Less; but that he
who loves can only love with the whole heart,
and with the whole soul; with all his strength
and with all his will.

But, alas, how little remains of this love by
the time we have finished one-half of our life-
journey! Soon the child learns that there are
strangers, and ceases to be a child. The spring
of love becomes hidden and soon filled up. Our
eyes gleam no more, and heavy-hearted we pass
one another in the bustling streets. We scarcely
greet each other, for we know how sharply it cuts
the soul when a greeting remains unanswered,
and how sad it is to be sundered from those
whom we have once greeted, and whose hands
we have clasped. The wings of the soul lose
their plumes; the leaves of the flower fast fall

off and wither; and of this fountain of love
there remain but a few drops. We still call
these few drops love, but it is no longer the
clear, fresh, all-abounding child-love. It is love
with anxiety and trouble, a consuming flame, a
burning passion; love which wastes itself like
rain-drops upon the hot sand; love which is a
longing, not a sacrifice; love which says "Wilt
thou be mine," not love which says, "I *must* be
thine." It is a most selfish, vacillating love.
And this is the love which poets sing and in
which young men and maidens believe; a fire
which burns up and down, yet does not warm,
and leaves nothing behind but smoke and ashes.
All of us at some period of life have believed
that these rockets of sunbeams were everlasting
love, but the brighter the glitter, the darker the
night which follows.

And then when all around grows dark, when
we feel utterly alone, when all men right and left
pass us by and know us not, a forgotten feeling
rises in the breast. We know not what it is, for

it is neither love nor friendship. You feel like crying to him who passes you so cold and strange: "Dost thou not know me?" Then one realizes that man is nearer to man than brother to brother, father to son, or friend to friend. How an old, holy saying rings through our souls, that strangers are nearest to us. Why must we pass them in silence? We know not, but must resign ourselves to it. When two trains are rushing by upon the iron rails and thou seest a well-known eye that would recognize thee, stretch out thy hand and try to grasp the hand of a friend, and perhaps thou wilt understand why man passes man in silence here below.

An old sage says: "I saw the fragments of a wrecked boat floating on the sea. Only a few meet and hold together a long time. Then comes a storm and drives them east and west, and here below they will never meet again. So it is with mankind. Yet no one has seen the great shipwreck."

THIRD MEMORY

THIRD MEMORY.

THE clouds in the sky of childhood do not last long, and disappear after a short, warm tear-rain. I was shortly again at the castle, and the Princess gave me her hand to kiss and then brought her children, the young princes and princesses, and we played together, as if we had known each other for years. Those were happy days when, after school—for I was now attending school—I could go to the castle and play. We had everything the heart could wish. I found playthings there which my mother had shown me in the shop-windows, and which were so dear, she told me, that poor people could live a whole week on what they cost. When I begged the Princess' permission to take them home and show them to my mother, she was perfectly willing. I could turn over and over and

look for hours at a time at beautiful picture
books, which I had seen in the book stores with
my father, but which were made only for very
good children. Everything which belonged to
the young princes belonged also to me — so I
thought, at least. Furthermore, I was not only
allowed to carry away what I wished, but I often
gave away the playthings to other children. In
short, I was a young Communist, in the full sense
of the term. I remember at one time the Princess had a golden snake which coiled itself
around her arm as if it were alive, and she gave
it to us for a plaything. As I was going home I
put the snake on my arm and thought I would
give my mother a real fright with it. On the
way, however, I met a woman who noticed the
snake and begged me to show it to her; and then
she said if she could only keep the golden snake,
she could release her husband from prison with
it. Naturally I did not stop to think for a minute, but ran away and left the woman alone with
the golden serpent-bracelet. The next day

there was much excitement. The poor woman was brought to the castle and the people said she had stolen it. Thereupon I grew very angry and explained with holy zeal that I had given her the bracelet and that I would not take it back again. What further occurred I know not, but I remember that after that time, I showed the Princess everything I took home with me.

It was a long time before my conceptions of Meum and Tuum were fully settled, and at a very late period they were at times confused, just as it was a long time before I could distinguish between the blue and red colors. The last time I remember my friends laughing at me on this account was when my mother gave me some money to buy apples. She gave me a groschen. The apples cost only a sechser, and when I gave the woman the groschen, she said, very sadly as it seemed to me, that she had sold nothing the whole livelong day and could not give me back a sechser. She wished I would buy a groschen's worth. Then it occurred to me that I also had

a sechser in my pocket, and thoroughly delighted
that I had solved the difficult problem, I gave it
to the woman and said: "Now you can give me
back a sechser." She understood me so little
however that she gave me back the groschen and
kept the sechser.

At this time, while I was making almost daily
visits to the young princes at the castle, both to
play as well as to study French with them,
another image comes up in my memory. It was
the daughter of the Princess, the Countess Marie.
The mother died shortly after the birth of the
child and the Prince subsequently married a second time. I know not when I saw her for the
first time. She emerges from the darkness of
memory slowly and gradually—at first like an
airy shadow which grows more and more distinct
as it approaches nearer and nearer, at last standing before my soul like the moon, which on some
stormy night throws back the cloud-veils from
across its face. She was always sick and suffering and silent, and I never saw her except reclin-

ing upon her couch, upon which two servants
brought her into the room and carried her out
again, when she was tired.   There she lay in her
flowing white drapery, with her hands generally
folded   Her face was so pale and yet so mild,
and her eyes so deep and unfathomable, that
I often stood before her lost in thought and
looked upon her and asked myself if she was not
one of the "strange people" also.   Many a time
she placed her hand upon my head and then it
seemed to me that a thrill ran through all my
limbs and that I could not move or speak, but
must forever gaze into her deep, unfathomable
eyes.   She conversed very little with us, but
watched our sports, and when at times we grew
very noisy and quarrelsome, she did not complain but held her white hands over her brow
and closed her eyes as if sleeping.   But there
were days when she said she felt better, and on
such days she sat up on her couch, conversed
with us and told us curious stories.   I do not
know how old she was at that time.   She was so

helpless that she seemed like a child, and yet was so serious and silent that she could not have been one. When people alluded to her they involuntarily spoke gently and softly. They called her "the angel," and I never heard anything said of her that was not good and lovely. Often when I saw her lying so silent and helpless, and thought that she would never walk again in life, that there was for her neither work nor joy, that they would carry her here and there upon her couch until they laid her upon her eternal bed of rest, I asked myself why she had been sent into this world, when she could have rested so gently on the bosom of the angels and they could have borne her through the air on their white wings, as I had seen in some sacred pictures. Again I felt as if I must take a part of her burden, so that she need not carry it alone, but we with her. I could not tell her all this for I knew it was not proper. I had an indefinable feeling. It was not a desire to embrace her. No one could have done that, for it would have wronged her. It seemed to me as if I could pray from the very bottom of my heart that she might be released from her burden.

One warm spring day she was brought into our room. She looked exceedingly pale; but her eyes were deeper and brighter than ever, and she sat upon her couch and called us to her. "It is my birth-day," said she, "and I was confirmed early this morning. Now, it is possible," she continued as she looked upon her father with a smile, "that God may soon call me to him, although I would gladly remain with you much longer. But if I am to leave you, I desire that you should not wholly forget me; and, therefore, I have brought a ring for each of you, which you must now place upon the fore-finger. As you grow older you can continue to change it until it fits the little finger; but you must wear it for your lifetime."

With these words she took the five rings she wore upon her fingers, which she drew off, one after the other, with a look so sad and yet so

affectionate, that I pressed my eyes closely to
keep from weeping. She gave the first ring to
her eldest brother and kissed him, the second
and third to the two princesses, and the fourth
to the youngest prince, and kissed them all as
she gave them the rings. I stood near by, and,
looking fixedly at her white hand, saw that she
still had a ring upon her finger; but she leaned
back and appeared wearied. My eyes met hers,
and as the eyes of a child speak so loudly, she
must have easily known my thoughts. I would
rather not have had the last ring, for I felt that I
was a stranger; that I did not belong to her, and
that she was not as affectionate to me as to her
brothers and sisters. Then came a sharp pain
in my breast as if a vein had burst or a nerve
had been severed, and I knew not which way to
turn to conceal my anguish.

She soon raised herself again, placed her
hand upon my forehead and looked down into
my heart so deeply that I felt I had not a
thought invisible to her. She slowly drew the

last ring from her finger, gave it to me and said:
"I intended to have taken this with me, when I
went from you, but it is better you should wear
it and think of me when I am no longer with
you. Read the words engraved upon the ring:
'As God wills.' You have a passionate heart,
easily moved. May life subdue but not harden
it." Then she kissed me as she had her brothers
and gave me the ring.

All my feelings I do not truly know. I had
then grown up to boyhood, and the mild beauty
of the suffering angel could not linger in my
young heart without alluring it. I loved her as
only a boy can love, and boys love with an in-
tensity and truth and purity which few preserve
in their youth and manhood; but I believed she
belonged to the "strange people" to whom you
are not allowed to speak of love. I scarcely understood the earnest words she spoke to me. I
only felt that her soul was as near to mine as one
human soul can be to another. All bitterness
was gone from my heart. I felt myself no longer

4

alone, no longer a stranger, no longer shut out.
I was by her, with her and in her.   I thought it
might be a sacrifice for her to give me the ring,
and that she might have preferred to take it to
the grave with her, and a feeling arose in my
soul which overshadowed all other feelings, and
I said with quivering voice: "Thou must keep
the ring if thou dost not wish to give it to me;
for what is thine is mine."   She looked at me a
moment surprised and thoughtfully.   Then she
took the ring, placed it on her finger, kissed me
once more on the forehead, and said gently to
me: "Thou knowest not what thou sayest.
Learn to understand thyself.   Then shalt thou
be happy and make many others happy."

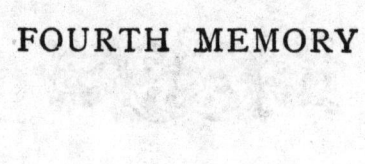

FOURTH MEMORY

FOURTH MEMORY.

EVERY life has its years in which one pro-
gresses as on a tedious and dusty street of
poplars, without caring to know where he is. Of
these years nought remains in memory but the
sad feeling that we have advanced and only
grown older. While the river of life glides along
smoothly, it remains the same river; only the
landscape on either bank seems to change. But
then come the cataracts of life. They are firmly
fixed in memory, and even when we are past
them and far away, and draw nearer and nearer
to the silent sea of eternity, even then it seems
as if we heard from afar their rush and roar.
We feel that the life-force which yet remains and
impels us onward still has its source and supply
from those cataracts.

School time was ended, the first fleeting years
of university life were over, and many beautiful
life-dreams were over also.   But one of them
still remained: Faith in God and man.   Otherwise life would have been circumscribed within
one's narrow brain.   Instead of that, a nobler
consecration had preserved all, and even the
painful and incomprehensible events of life became a proof to me of the omnipresence of the
divine in the earthly.   "The least important
thing does not happen except as God wills it."
This was the brief life-wisdom I had accumulated.

During the summer holidays I returned to my
little native city.   What joy in these meetings
again!   No one has explained it, but in this seeing and finding again, and in these self-memories,
lie the real secrets of all joy and pleasure.   What
we see, hear or taste for the first time may be
beautiful, grand and agreeable, but it is too new.
It overpowers, but gives no repose, and the
fatigue of enjoying is greater than the enjoyment

itself. To hear again, years afterward, an old melody, every note of which we supposed we had forgotten, and yet to recognize it as an old acquaintance; or, after the lapse of many years, to stand once more before the Sistine Madonna at Dresden, and experience afresh all the emotions which the infinite look of the child aroused in us for years; or to smell a flower or taste a dish again which we have not thought of since childhood — all these produce such an intense charm that we do not know which we enjoy most, the actual pleasure or the old memory. So when we return again, after long absence, to our birth-place, the soul floats unconsciously in a sea of memories, and the dancing waves dreamily toss themselves upon the shores of times long passed. The belfry clock strikes and we fear we shall be late to school, and recovering from this fear feel relieved that our anxiety is over. The same dog runs along the street on whose account we used to go far out of our way. Here sits the old huckster whose apples often led us into temptation, and

even now, we fancy they must taste better than
all other apples in the world, notwithstanding the
dust on them.   There one has torn down a house
and built a new one.   Here the old music-
teacher lived.   He is dead — and yet how beautiful it seemed as we stood and listened on summer evenings under the window while the True
Soul, when the hours of the day were over, indulged in his own enjoyment and played fan-
tasies, like the roaring and hissing engine letting
off the steam which has accumulated during the
day.   Here in this little leafy lane, which seemed
at that time so much larger, as I was coming
home late one evening, I met our neighbor's
beautiful daughter.   At that time I had never
ventured to look at or address her, but we school-
children often spoke of her and called her "the
Beautiful Maiden," and whenever I saw her passing along the street at a distance I was so happy
that I could only think of the time when I should
meet her nearer.   Here in this leafy walk which
leads to the church-yard, I met her one evening

and she took me by the arm, although we had never spoken together before, and asked me to go home with her. I believe neither of us spoke a word the whole way; but I was so happy that even now, after all these years, I wish it were that evening, and that I could go home again, silently and blissfully, with "the Beautiful Maiden."

Thus one memory follows another until the waves dash together over our heads, and a deep sigh swells the breast, which warns us that we have forgotten to breathe in the midst of these pure thoughts. Then all at once, the whole dream-world vanishes, like uprisen ghosts at the crowing of the cock.

As I passed by the old castle and the lindens, and saw the sentinels upon their horses, how many memories awakened in my soul, and how everything had changed! Many years had flown since I was at the castle. The Princess was dead. The Prince had given up his rule and gone back to Italy, and the oldest prince, with whom I had grown up, was regent. His

companions were young noblemen and officers,
whose intercourse was congenial to him, and
whose company in our early days had often
estranged us.   Other circumstances combined
to weaken our young friendship. Like every
young man who perceives for the first time the
lack of unity in the German folk-life, and the
defects of German rule, I had caught up some
phrases of the Liberal party, which sounded as
strangely at court as unseemly expressions in an
honest minister's family. In short, it was many
years since I had ascended those stairs, and yet
a being dwelt in that castle whose name I had
named almost daily, and who was almost con-
stantly present in my memory. I had long dwelt
upon the thought that I should never see her
again in this life. She was transformed into an
image which I felt neither did nor could exist
in reality She had become my good angel —
my other self, to whom I talked instead of talking with myself. How she became so I could
not explain to myself, for I scarcely knew her.

Just as the eye sometimes pictures figures in the clouds, so I fancied my imagination had conjured up this sweet image in the heaven of my childhood, and a complete picture of phantasy developed itself out of the scarcely perceptible outlines of reality. My entire thought had involuntarily become a dialogue with her, and all that was good in me, all for which I struggled, all in which I believed, my entire better self, belonged to her. I gave it to her. I received it from her, from her my good angel.

I had been at home but a few days, when I received a letter one morning. It was written in English, and came from the Countess Marie:

Dear Friend: I hear you are with us for a short time. We have not met for many years, and if it is agreeable to you, I should like to see an old friend again. You will find me alone this afternoon in the Swiss Cottage.   Yours sincerely,

MARIE.

I immediately replied, also in English, that I would call in the afternoon.

The Swiss Cottage constituted a wing of the
castle, which overlooked the garden, and could
be reached without going through the castle
yard. It was five o'clock when I passed through
the garden and approached the cottage. I repressed all emotion and prepared myself for a
formal meeting. I sought to quiet my good
angel, and to assure her that this lady had
nothing to do with her. And yet I felt very
uneasy, and my good angel would not listen to
counsel. Finally I took courage, murmuring
something to myself about the masquerade of
life, and rapped on the door, which stood ajar.

There was no one in the room except a lady
whom I did not know, and who likewise spoke
English, and said the Countess would be present
in a moment. She then left, and I was alone,
and had time to look about.

The walls of the room were of rose-chestnut,
and over an openwork trellis, a luxuriant broad-
leaved ivy twined around the whole room. All
the tables and chairs were of carved rose-chest-

nut. The floor was of variegated woodwork. It gave me a curious sensation to see so much that was familiar in the room. Many articles from our old play-room in the castle were old friends, but the others were new, especially the pictures, and yet they were the same as those in my University room — the same portraits of Beethoven, Händel and Mendelssohn, as I had selected — hung over the grand piano. In one corner I saw the Venus di Milo, which I always regarded as the masterpiece of antiquity. On the table were volumes of Dante, Shakspeare, Tauler's Sermons, the "German Theology," Ruckert's Poems, Tennyson and Burns, and Carlyle's "Past and Present,"— the very same books— all of which I had had but recently in my hands. I was growing thoughtful, but I repressed my thoughts and was just standing before the portrait of the deceased Princess, when the door opened, and the same two servants, whom I had so often seen in childhood, brought the Countess into the room upon her couch.

What a vision! She spoke not a word, and her countenance was as placid as the sea, until the servants left the room. Then her eyes sought me — the old, deep, unfathomable eyes. Her expression grew more animated each instant. At last her whole face lit up, and she said:

"We are old friends — I believe; we have not changed. I cannot say 'You,' and if I may not say 'Thou,' then we must speak in English. Do you understand me?"

I had not anticipated such a reception, for I saw here was no masquerade — here was a soul which longed for another soul — here was a greeting like that between two friends who recognize each other by the glance of the eye, notwithstanding their disguises and dark masks. I seized the hand she held out to me, and replied: "When we address an angel, we cannot say 'You.'"

And yet how singular is the influence of the forms and habits of life! How difficult it is to speak the language of nature even to the most

congenial souls! Our conversation halted, and
both of us felt the embarrassment of the moment.
I broke the silence and spoke out my thoughts:
"Men become accustomed to live from youth
up as it were in a cage, and when they are once
in the open air they dare not venture to use their
wings, fearing, if they fly, that they may stumble
against everything."

"Yes," replied she, "and that is very proper
and cannot well be otherwise. One often wishes
that he could live like the birds which fly in the
woods, and meet upon the branches and sing
together without being presented to each other.
But, my friend, even among the birds there are
owls and sparrows, and in life it is well that one
can pass them without knowing them. It is
sometimes with life as with poetry. As the real
poet can express the Truest and most Beautiful,
although fettered by metrical form, so man
should know how to preserve freedom of thought
and feeling notwithstanding the restraints of
society."

I could not help recalling the words of
Platen : "That which proves itself everlasting
under all circumstances, told in the fetters of
words, is the unfettered spirit."

"Yes," said she, with a cordial but sweetly
playful smile; "but I have a privilege which is
at the same time my burden and loneliness. I
often pity the young men and maidens, for they
cannot have a friendship or an intimacy without
their relatives or themselves pronouncing it love,
or what they call love. They lose much on this
account. The maiden knows not what slumbers
in her soul, and what might be awakened by
earnest conversation with a noble friend; and
the young man in turn would acquire so much
knightly virtue if women were suffered to be the
distant witnesses of the inner struggles of the
spirit. It will not do, however, for immediately
love comes in play, or what they call love — the
quick beating of the heart — the stormy billows
of hope — the delight over a beautiful face — the
sweet sentimentality — sometimes also prudent

calculation — in short, all that troubles the calm sea, which is the true picture of pure human love ——"

She checked herself suddenly, and an expression of pain passed over her countenance. "I dare not talk more to-day," said she; "my physician will not allow it. I would like to hear one of Mendelssohn's songs — that duet, which my young friend used to play years ago. Is it not so?"

I could not answer, for as she ceased speaking and gently folded her hands, I saw upon her hand a ring. She wore it on her little finger — the ring which she had given me and I had given her. Thoughts came too fast for utterance, and I seated myself at the piano and played. When I had done, I turned around and said: "Would one could only speak thus in tones without words!"

"That is possible," said she; "I understood it all. But I must not do anything more to-day, for every day I grow weaker. We must be better acquainted, and a poor sick recluse may certainly claim forbearance. We meet to-morrow evening, at the same hour; shall we not?"

I seized her hand and was about to kiss it, but she held my hand firmly, pressed it and said: "It is better thus. Good bye."

FIFTH MEMORY

FIFTH MEMORY.

IT would be difficult to describe my thoughts
and emotions as I went home. The soul
cannot at once translate itself perfectly in words,
and there are "thoughts without words," which
in every man are the prelude of supreme joy and
suffering. It was neither joy nor pain, only an
indescribable bewilderment which I felt; thoughts
flew through my innermost being like meteors,
which shoot from heaven towards earth but are
extinguished before they reach the goal. As we
sometimes say in a dream, "I am dreaming," so
I said to myself "thou livest"—"it is she." I
tried again to reflect and calm myself, and said,
"She is a lovely vision — a very wonderful spirit."
At another time, I pictured the delightful evenings I should pass during the holidays. But no,

no, this cannot be. She is everything I sought,
thought, hoped and believed. Here was at last
a human soul, as clear and fresh as a spring
morning. I had seen at the first glance what she
was and how she felt, and we had greeted and
recognized one another. And my good angel in
me, she answered me no more. She was gone
and I felt there was no place on earth where I
should find her again.

Now began a beautiful life, for I was with her
every evening. We soon realized that we were
in truth old acquaintances and that we could
only call each other *Thou.* It seemed also as if
we had lived near and with one another always,
for she manifested not an emotion that did not
find its counterpart in my soul, and there was no
thought which I uttered to which she did not
nod friendly assent, as much as to say: "I
thought so too." I had previously heard the
greatest master of our time and his sister extem-
porize on the piano, and scarcely comprehended
how two persons could understand and feel

themselves so perfectly and yet never, not even in a single note, disturb the harmony of their playing. Now it became intelligible to me. Yes, now I understood for the first time that my soul was not so poor and empty as it had seemed to me, and that it had been only the sun that was lacking to open all its germs and buds to the light. And yet what a sad and brief spring-time it was that our souls experienced! We forget in May that roses so soon wither, but here every evening reminded us that one leaf after another was falling to the ground. She felt it before I did, and alluded to it apparently without pain, and our interviews grew more earnest and solemn daily.

One evening, as I was about to leave, she said: "I did not think I should grow so old. When I gave you the ring on my confirmation day I thought I should have to take my departure from you all, very soon. And yet I have lived so many years, and enjoyed so much beauty — and suffered so very much! But one

forgets that! Now, while I feel that my departure is near, every hour, every minute,
grows precious to me. Good night! Do not
come too late to-morrow."

One day as I went into her room, I met an
Italian painter with her. She spoke Italian with
him, and although he was evidently more artisan
than artist, she addressed him with such amia-
bility and modesty, with such respect even, one
could not avoid recognizing that nobility of soul
which is the true nobility of birth. When the
painter had taken his leave, she said to me: "I
wish to show you a picture which will please
you. The original is in the gallery at Paris. I
read a description of it, and have had it copied
by the Italian." She showed me the painting,
and waited my opinion. It was a picture of a
man of middle age, in the old German costume.
The expression was dreamy and resigned, and so
characteristic that no one could doubt this man
once lived. The whole tone of the picture in
the foreground was dark and brownish; but in

the background was a landscape, and on the horizon the first gleams of daybreak appeared. I could discover nothing special in the picture, and yet it produced a feeling of such satisfaction that one might have tarried to look at it for hours at a time. "There is nothing like a genuine human face," said I; "Raphael himself could not have imagined a face like this."

"No," said she. "But now I will tell you why I wished to have the picture. I read that no one knew the artist, nor whom the picture represents. But it is very clearly a philosopher of the Middle Ages. Just such a picture I wanted for my gallery, for you are aware that no one knows the author of the 'German Theology,' and moreover, that we have no picture of him. I wished to try whether the picture of an Unknown by an Unknown would answer for our German theologian, and if you have no objections we will hang it here between the 'Albigenses' and the 'Diet of Worms,' and call it the 'German Theologian.'"

"Good," said I; "but it is somewhat too
vigorous and manly for the Frankforter."

"That may be," replied she. "But for a suffering and dying life like mine, much consolation
and strength may be derived from his book. I
thank him much, for it disclosed to me for the
first time the true secret of Christian doctrine
in all its simplicity. I felt that I was free to
believe or disbelieve the old teacher, whoever he
may have been, for his doctrines had no external
constraint upon me; at last it seized upon me
with such power that it seemed to me I knew
for the first time what revelation was. It is
precisely this fact that bars so many out from
true Christianity, namely: that its doctrines confront us as revelation before revelation takes
place in ourselves. This has often given me
much anxiety; not that I had ever doubted the
truth and divinity of our religion, but I felt I had
no right to a belief which others had given me,
and that what I had learned and received when
a child, without comprehending, did not belong

to me. One can believe for us as little as one can live and die for us."

"Certainly," said I; "therein lies the cause of many hot and bitter struggles; that the teachings of Christ, instead of winning our hearts gradually and irresistibly, as they won the hearts of the apostles and early Christians, confront us from the earliest childhood as the infallible law of a mighty church, and demand of us an unconditional submission, which they call faith. Doubts arise sooner or later in the breast of every one who has the power of thinking and reverence for the truth; and then even when we are on the right road, to overcome our faith, the terrors of doubt and unbelief arise and disturb the tranquil development of the new life."

"I read recently in an English work," she interrupted, "that truth makes revelation, and not revelation truth. This perfectly expressed what I found in reading the 'German Theology.' I read the book, and I felt the power of its truths so overwhelmingly that I was compelled to submit to it. The truth was revealed to me; or rather, I was revealed to myself, and I felt for the first time what belief meant. The truth which had long slumbered in my soul belonged to me, but it was the word of the unknown teacher which filled me with light, illuminated my inner vision, and brought out my indistinct presentiments in fuller clearness before my soul. When I had thus experienced for the first time how the human soul can believe, I read the Gospels as if they, too, had been written by an unknown man, and banished the thought as well as I could that they were an inspiration from the Holy Ghost to the apostles, in some wonderful manner; that they had been endorsed by the councils and proclaimed by the church as the supreme authority of the alone-saving belief. Then, for the first time, I understood what Christian faith and revelation were."

"It is wonderful," said I, "that the theologians have not broken down all religion, and they will succeed yet, if the believers do not

seriously confront them and say: 'Thus far but
no farther.' Every church must have its servants, but there has been as yet no religion
which the Priests, the Brahmins, the Schamins,
the Bonzes, the Lamas, the Pharisees, or the
Scribes have not corrupted and perverted. They
wrangle and dispute in a language unintelligible
to nine-tenths of their congregations, and instead
of permitting themselves to be inspired by the
apostles, and of inspiring others with their inspiration, they construct long arguments to show
that the Gospels must be true, because they
were written by inspired men. But this is only
a makeshift for their own unbelief. How can
they know that these men were inspired in a
wonderful mañner, without ascribing to themselves a still more wonderful inspiration? Therefore they extend the gift of inspiration to the
fathers of the church; they attribute to them
those very things which the majority have incor-
porated in the canons of the councils; and there
again, when the question arises how we know

that of fifty bishops twenty-six were inspired
and twenty-four were not, they finally take the
last desperate step, and say that infallibility and
inspiration are inherent in the heads of the
church down to the present day, through the
laying on of hands, so that infallibility, majority
and inspiration make all our convictions, all
resignation, all devout intuitions, superfluous.
And yet, notwithstanding all these connecting
links, the first question returns in all its simplicity: How can B know that A is inspired, if B
is not equally, or even more, inspired than A?
For it is of more consequence to know that A
was inspired than for one's self to be inspired."

"I have never comprehended this so clearly
myself," said she. "But I have often felt how
difficult it must be to know whether one loves
who shows not a sign of love that could not be
imitated. And, again, I have thought that no
one could know it unless he knew love himself,
and that he could only believe in the love of
another so far as he believed in his own love.

As with the gift of love so is it with the gift of
the Holy Spirit. They upon whom it descended
heard a rushing from heaven as of a mighty
wind, and there appeared to them cloven tongues
like as of fire. But the rest were either amazed
and perplexed, or they made sport of them and
said : ' They are full of sweet wine.'

"Still, as I said to you, it is the ' German
Theology ' to which I am indebted for learning
to believe in my belief, and what will seem a
weakness to many, strengthened me the most;
namely, that the old master never stops to dem-
onstrate his propositions rigidly, but scatters
them like a sower, in the hope that some grains
will fall upon good soil and bear fruit a thousand
fold. So our Divine Master never attempted to
prove his doctrines, for the perfect conviction of
truth disdains the form of a demonstration."

"Yes," I interrupted her, for I could not help
thinking of the wonderful chain of proof in
Spinoza's 'Ethics,' "the straining after demonstration by Spinoza gives me the impression that

this acute thinker could not have believed in his
own doctrines with his whole heart, and that he
therefore felt the necessity of fastening every
mesh of his net with the utmost care. " Still," I
continued, " I must acknowledge I do not share
this great admiration for the 'German Theology,'
although I owe the book many a doubt. To me
there is a lack of the human and the poetical in
it, and of warm feeling and reverence for reality
altogether. The entire mysticism of the four-
teenth century is wholesome as a preparative, but
it first reaches solution in the divinely holy and
divinely courageous return to real life, as was
exemplified by Luther. Man must at some time
in his life recognize his nothingness. He must
feel that he is nothing of himself, that his existence, his beginning, his everlasting life are rooted
in the superearthly and incomprehensible. That
is the returning to God which in reality is never
concluded on earth but yet leaves behind in the
soul a divine home sickness, which never again
ceases. But man cannot ignore the creation as the

Mystics would. Although created out of nothing, that is, through and out of God, he cannot of his own power resolve himself back into this nothingness. The self-annihilation of which Tauler so often speaks is scarcely better than the sinking away of the human soul in Nirvana, as the Buddhists have it. Thus Tauler says: 'That if he by greater reverence and love could reach the highest existence in non-existence, he would willingly sink from his height into the deepest abyss.' But this annihilation of the creature was not the purpose of the Creator since he made it. 'God is transformed in man,' says Augustine, 'not man in God.' Thus mysticism should be only a fire-trial which steels the soul but does not evaporate it like boiling water in a kettle. He who has recognized the nothingness of self ought to recognize this self as a reflection of the actual divine. The 'German Theology' says:

[„Was nu us geflossen ist, das ist nicht war wesen, und hat kein wesen anders dan in dem volkomen, sunder es ist ein zufal oder ein glast und ein
6

ſchin, der nicht weſen iſt oder nicht weſen hat anders,
dan in dem ſewer, da der glaſt us fluſſet, als in der
ſunnen oder in einem liechte."]

"What has flown out is not real substance
and has no other reality except in the perfect;
but it is an incident or a glare or a shimmer,
which is no substance, and has no other reality,
except in the fire from which a glare proceeds,
as in the sun or a light."

"What is emitted from the divine, though it
be only like the reflection from the fire, still has
the divine reality in itself, and one might almost
ask what were the fire without glow, the sun without light, or the Creator without the creature?
These are questions of which it is said very
truthfully :

[„Welch menſche und welche creatur begert zu erfa-
ren und zu wiſſen den heimlichen rat und willen
gottes, der begert nicht anders denne als Adam tet
und der böſe geiſt."]

"What man or creature desires to learn and
to know the secret counsel and will of God —

desires nothing else but what Adam did and the
evil spirit.

"For this reason, it should be enough for us
to feel and to appear that we are a reflection of
the divine until we are divine. No one should
place under a bushel or extinguish the divine
light which illuminates us, but let it beam out,
that it may brighten and warm all about it. Then
one feels a living fire in his veins, and a higher
consecration for the struggle of life. The most
trivial duties remind us of God. The earthly
becomes divine, the temporal eternal, and our
entire life a life in God. God is not eternal
repose. He is everlasting life, which Angelus
Silesius forgets when he says: 'God is without
will.'

> 'We pray: 'Thy will my Lord and God be done,'
> And lo, He has no will! He is an eternal silence.'"

She listened to me quietly, and, after a moment's reflection, said: "Health and strength
belong to your faith; but there are life-weary

souls, who long for rest and sleep, and feel so
lonely that when they fall asleep in God, they
miss the world as little as the world misses them.
It is a foretaste of divine rest to them when they
can wrap themselves in the divine; and this they
can do, since no tie binds them fast to earth, and
no wish troubles their hearts except the wish for
rest.

> 'Rest is the highest good, and were God not rest,
> Then would I avert my gaze even from Him.'

"You do the German theologian an injustice.
It is true he teaches the nothingness of the
external life, but he does not wish to see it annihilated.   Read me the twenty-eighth chapter."

I took the book and read, while she closed
her eyes and listened:

[,,Und wa die voreinunge geschicht in der wahrheit
und wesentlich wirt, da stet vorbaß der inner mensche
in der einung unbeweglich und got leßt den ussern
menschen her und dar bewegt werden von diesem zu
dem. Das muß und sol sin und geschehen, daß der
usser mensche spricht und es ouch in der warheit also

ist, „ich wil weder sin noch nit sin, weder leben oder
sterben, wißen oder nicht wißen, tun oder laßen,
und alles das disem glich ist, sunder alles, das da
muß und sol sin und geschehen, da bin ich bereit
und gehorsam zu, es si in libender wise oder in
tuender wise." Und alsoe hat der ußer mensch kein
warumbe oder gesuch, sunder alleine dem ewigen
willen genuk zu sin. Wan das wirt bekannt in der
warheit, das der inner mensche sten sol unbeweglich
und der ußer mensch muß und sol bewegt werden,
und hat der inner mensch in siner beweglikeit ein
warumb, das ist anders nichts dann ein muß= und
sol=sin, geordnet von dem ewigen willen. Und wa
got selber der mensch were oder ist, da ist es also.
Das merket man wol in Kristo. Duch wa das in
götlichem und us götlichem liechte ist, da ist nit geist=
liche hochfart noch unachtsame friheit oder frie gemute,
sunder ein gruntlose bemutigkeit und ein nider ge=
schlagen und ein gesunken betrubet gemut, und alle
ordenligkeit und redeligkeit, glichheit und warheit,
fride und genugsamkeit, und alles das, das allen
tugenden zu gehört, das muß da sin. Wa es anders
ist, da ist im nit recht, als vor gesprochen ist. Wan
recht als dises oder das zu diser einung nit gehelfen
oder gedienen kan, also ist ouch nichtes, das es geirren
oder gehindern mag, denn alleine der mensch mit

ſinem eigen willen, der tut im diſen groſßen ſchaden.
Das ſol man wiſſen."]

"And when the union takes place in truth
and becomes real, then the inner man stands
henceforth immovable in the union, and God
permits the outer man to be driven hither and
thither from this to that. It must and shall be
and happen, that the outer man says — and is so
also in truth —'I will neither be nor not be,
neither live nor die, neither know nor not know,
neither do nor leave undone — and everything
which is similar to this, but I am ready and
obedient to do everything, which must and shall
be done, be it passively or actively.' And thus
has the outer man no question or desire, but to
satisfy only the Eternal Will. When this will be
known in truth, that the inner man shall stand
immovable, and that the outer man shall and
must be moved,— the inner man has a why and
wherefore of his moving, which is nothing but
an 'it must and shall be' ordered by the Eternal
Will. And if God himself were or is the man,
it would be so. This is well seen in Christ.
And what in the Divine Light is and from the
Divine Light, has neither spiritual pride nor

careless license nor an independent spirit — but
a great humility, and a broken and contrite
heart,— and all propriety and honesty, justice
and truth, peace and happiness,— all that be-
longs to all virtues, it must have. When it is
otherwise, then he is not happy, as has been
said. When this does not help to this union,
then there is nothing which may hinder it but
man alone with his own will, which does him
such great harm. That, one ought to know."

"This is sufficient," said she; "I believe we
understand each other now. In another place,
our unknown friend says still more unmistakably
that no man is passive before death, and that the
glorified man is like the hand of God, which
does nothing of itself except as God wills; or,
like a house in which God dwells. A God-
possessed man feels this perfectly, but does not
speak of it. He treasures his life in God like
a love secret. It often seems to me like that
silver poplar before my window. It is perfectly
still at evening, and not a leaf trembles or stirs.
When the morning breeze rustles and tosses

every leaf, the trunk with its branches stands still
and immovable, and when autumn comes, though
every leaf which once rustled falls to the ground
and withers, the trunk waits for a new spring."

She had lived so deep a life in her world that
I did not wish to disturb it. I had but just released myself with difficulty from the magic
circle of these thoughts, and scarcely knew
whether she had not chosen the better part
which could not be taken away from her; while
we have so much trouble and care.

Thus every evening brought its new conversation, and with each evening, some new phase of
her fathomless mind disclosed itself. She kept
no secret from me. Her talk was only thinking
and feeling aloud, and what she said must have
dwelt with her many long years, for she poured
out her thoughts as freely as a child that picks
its lap full of flowers and then sprinkles them
upon the grass. I could not disclose my soul to
her as freely as she did to me, and this oppressed
and pained me. Yet how few can, with those

continual deceptions imposed upon us by society, called manners, politeness, consideration, prudence, and worldly wisdom, which make our entire life a masquerade! How few, even when they would, can regain the complete truth of their existence! Love itself dares not speak its own language and maintain its own silence, but must learn the set phrases of the poet and idealize, sigh and flirt instead of freely greeting, beholding and surrendering itself. I would most gladly have confessed and said to her: "You know me not," but I found that the words were not wholly true. Before I left, I gave her a volume of Arnold's poems, which I had had a short time, and begged her to read the one called "The Buried Life." It was my confession, and then I kneeled at her couch and said "Good Night." "Good Night," said she, and laid her hand upon my head, and again her touch thrilled through every limb and the dreams of childhood uprose in my soul. I could not go, but gazed into her deep unfathomable eyes until the peace of her soul

completely overshadowed mine. Then I arose
and went home in silence — and in the night I
dreamed of the silver poplar around which the
wind roared — but not a leaf stirred on its
branches.

THE BURIED LIFE.

Light flows our war of mocking words, and yet
Behold, with tears my eyes are wet;
I feel a nameless sadness o'er me roll.
　　Yes, yes, we know that we can jest;
We know, we know that we can smile;
But there's a something in this breast
To which thy light words bring no rest,
And thy gay smiles no anodyne.
　　Give me thy hand, and hush awhile,
And turn those limpid eyes on mine,
And, let me read there, love, thy inmost soul.
　　Alas, is even love too weak
To unlock the heart, and let it speak?
Are even lovers powerless to reveal
To one another what indeed they feel?
I knew the mass of men concealed
Their thoughts, for fear that if revealed

They would by other men be met
With blank indifference, or with blame reproved;
I knew they lived and moved,
Tricked in disguises, alien to the rest
Of men and alien to themselves—and yet,
The same heart beats in every human breast.

But we, my love—does a like spell benumb
Our hearts—our voices?—must we too be dumb?
Ah! well for us, if even we,
Even for a moment, can yet free
Our hearts and have our lips unchained:
For that which seals them hath been deep ordained.
Fate which foresaw
How frivolous a baby man would be,
By what distractions he would be possessed,
How he would pour himself in every strife,
And well-nigh change his own identity,
That it might keep from his capricious play
His genuine self, and force him to obey,
Even in his own despite, his being's law,
Bade through the deep recesses of our breast
The unregarded River of our Life,
Pursue with indiscernible flow its way;
And that we should not see
The buried stream, and seem to be

Eddying about in blind uncertainty,
Though driving on with it eternally.

But often, in the world's most crowded streets,
But often in the din of strife,
There rises an unspeakable desire
After the knowledge of our buried life;
A thirst to spend our fire and restless force
In tracking out our true original course;
A longing to inquire
Into the mystery of this heart that beats
So wild, so deep, in us; to know
Whence our thoughts come, and where they go.
And many a man in his own breast then delves,
But deep enough, alas, none ever mines:
And we have been on many thousand lines,
And we have shown on each, talent and power,
But hardly have we, for one little hour,
Been on our own line, have we been ourselves;
Hardly had skill to utter one of all
The nameless feelings that course through our breast
But they course on forever unexpressed.
And long we try in vain to speak and act
Our hidden self, and what we say and do
Is eloquent, is well—but 'tis not true.

But then we will no more be racked

With inward striving, and demand
Of all the thousand nothings of the hour
Their stupefying power;
Ah! yes, and they benumb us at our call.
Yet still, from time to time, vague and forlorn,
From the soul's subterranean depth upborne,
As from an infinitely distant land,
Come airs and floating echoes, and convey
A melancholy into all our day.
   Only — but this is rare —
When a beloved hand is laid in ours,
When, jaded with the rush and glare
Of the interminable hours,
Our eyes can in another's eyes read clear,
When our world-deafened ear
Is by the tones of a loved voice caressed,—
A bolt is shot back somewhere in our breast,
And a lost pulse of feeling stirs again:
The eye sinks inward, and the heart lies plain,
And what we mean, we say, and what we would, we
     know;
A man becomes aware of his life's flow,
And hears its winding murmur, and he sees
The meadows where it glides, the sun, the breeze.
   And there arrives a lull in the hot race

Wherein he doth forever chase
That flying and elusive shadow, Rest;
An air of coolness plays upon his face,
And an unwonted calm pervades his breast.
　　And then he thinks he knows
　　The Hills where his life rose,
　　And the Sea where it goes. . . . . . .

SIXTH MEMORY

SIXTH MEMORY.

EARLY the next morning, there was a knock
at the door, and my old doctor, the Hofrath,
entered. He was the friend, the body-and-soul-
guardian of our entire little village. He had
seen two generations grow up. Children whom
he had brought into the world had in turn become fathers and mothers, and he treated them
as his children. He himself was unmarried, and
even in his old age was strong and handsome to
look upon. I never knew him otherwise than as
he stood before me at that time; his clear blue
eyes gleaming under the bushy brows, his flowing white hair still full of youthful strength, curl-
ing and vigorous. I can never forget, also, his
shoes, with their silver buckles, his white stock-
ings, his brown coat, which always looked new,
and yet seemed to be old, and his cane, which

was the same I had seen standing by my bedside
in childhood, when he felt my pulse and pre-
scribed my medicines. I had often been sick,
but it was always faith in this man which made
me well again.   I never had the slightest doubt
of his ability to cure me, and when my mother
said she must send for the Hofrath that I might
get well again, it was as if she had said she must
send for the tailor to mend my torn trousers.
I had only to take the medicine, and I felt that
I *must* be well again.

"How are you, my child?" said he, as he
entered the room. "You are not looking perfectly well. You must not study too much. But
I have little time to-day to talk, and only came
to tell you, you must not go to see the Countess
Marie again. I have been with her all night,
and it is your fault. So be careful, if her life is
dear to you, that you do not go again. She
must leave here as soon as possible, and be
taken into the country. It would be best for

you also to travel for a long time. So good morning, and be a good child."

With these words, he gave me his hand, looked at me affectionately in the eyes, as if he would exact the promise, and then went on his way to look after his sick children.

I was so astonished that another had penetrated so deeply into the secrets of my soul, and that he knew what I did not know myself, that when I recovered from it he had already been long upon the street. An agitation began to seize me, as water, which has long been over the fire without stirring, suddenly bubbles up, boils, heaves and rages until it overflows.

Not see her again! I only live when I am with her. I will be calm; I will not speak a word to her; I will only stand at her window as she sleeps and dreams. But not to see her again! Not to take one farewell from her! She knows not, they cannot know, that I love her. Surely I do not love her—I desire nothing, I hope for nothing, my heart never beats more quietly then when I am with her. But I must feel her presence — I must breathe her spirit — I must go to her! She waits for me. Has destiny thrown us together without design? Ought I not to be her consolation, and ought she not to be my repose? Life is not a sport. It does not force two souls together like the grains of sand in the desert, which the sirocco whirls together and then asunder. We should hold fast the souls which friendly fate leads to us, for they are destined for us, and no power can tear them from us if we have the courage to live, to struggle, and to die for them. She would despise me if I deserted her love at the first roll of the thunder, as it were in the shadow of a tree, under which I have dreamed so many happy hours.

Then I suddenly grew calm, and heard only the words "her love;" they reverberated through all the recesses of my soul like an echo, and I was terrified at myself. "Her love," and how had I deserved it? She hardly knows me, and even if she could love me, must I not confess to her I do not deserve the love of an angel? Every thought, every hope which arose in my soul, fell back like a bird which essays to soar into the blue sky and does not see the wires which restrain it. And yet, why all this bliss-fulness, so near and so unattainable? Cannot God work wonders? Does He not work won-ders every morning? Has He not often heard my prayer when it importuned him, and would not cease, until consolation and help came to the weary one? These are not earthly blessings for which we pray. It is only that two souls, which have found and recognized each other, may be allowed to finish their brief life-journey, arm in arm, and face to face; that I may be a support to her in suffering, and that she may be a consolation and precious burden to me until we reach the end. And if a still later spring were promised to her life, if her burdens were taken from her—Oh, what blissful scenes crowded upon my vision! The castle of her deceased mother, in the Tyrol, belonged to her. There,

on the green mountains, in the fresh mountain
air, among a sturdy and uncorrupted people, far
away from the hurly-burly of the world, its cares
and its struggles, its opinion and its censure,
how blissfully we could await the close of life,
and silently fade away like the evening-red!
Then I pictured the dark lake, with the dancing
shimmer of waves, and the clear shadows of distant glaciers reflected in it; I heard the lowing
of cattle and the songs of the herdsmen; I saw
the hunters with their rifles crossing the mountains, and the old and young gathering together
at twilight in the village; and, to crown all, I saw
her passing along like an angel of peace in bene-
diction, and I was her guide and friend. "Poor
fool!" I cried out, "poor fool! Is thy heart
always to be so wild and so weak? Be a man.
Think who thou art, and how far thou art from
her. She is a friend. She gladly reflects herself in another's soul, but her childlike trust and
candor at best only show that no deeper feeling
lives in her breast for thee. Hast thou not, on

many a clear summer's night, wandering alone
through the beech groves, seen how the moon
sheds its light upon all the branches and leaves,
how it brightens the dark, dull water of the pool
and reflects itself clearly in the smallest drops?
In like manner she shines upon this dark life,
and thou may'st feel her gentle radiance reflected in thy heart — but hope not for a warmer
glow!"

Suddenly an image approached me as it were
from life; she stood before me, not like a memory but as a vision, and I realized for the first
time how beautiful she was. It was not that
beauty of form and face which dazzles us at the
first sight of a lovely maiden, and then fades
away as suddenly as a blossom in spring. It was
much more the harmony of her whole being, the
reality of every emotion, the spirituality of expression, the perfect union of body and soul
which blesses him so who looks upon it. The
beauty which nature lavishes so prodigally does
not bring any satisfaction, if the person is not

adapted to it and as it were deserves and over-
comes it. On the other hand, it is offensive, as
when we look upon an actress striding along the
stage in queenly costume, and notice at every
step how poorly the attire fits her, how little it
becomes her. True beauty is sweetness, and
sweetness is the spiritualizing of the gross, the
corporeal and the earthly. It is the spiritual
presence which transforms ugliness into beauty.
The more I looked upon the vision which stood
before me, the more I perceived, above all else,
the majestic beauty of her person and the soul-
ful depths of her whole being. Oh, what happiness was near me! And was this all — to be
shown the summit of earthly bliss and then be
thrust out into the flat, sandy wastes of existence?
Oh, that I had never known what treasures the
earth conceals! Once to love, and then to be
forever alone! Once to believe, and then forever
to doubt! Once to see the light, and then forever to be blinded! In comparison with this

rack, all the torture-chambers of man are insignificant.

Thus rushed the wild chase of my thoughts farther and farther away until at last all was silent. The confused sensations gradually collected and settled. This repose and exhaustion they call meditation, but it is rather an inspection —one allows time for the mixture of thoughts to crystallize themselves according to eternal laws, and regards the process like an observing chemist; and the elements having assumed a form, we often wonder that they, as well as ourselves, are so entirely different from what we expected.

When I awoke from my abstraction, my first words were, "I must away." I immediately sat down and wrote the Hofrath that I should travel for fourteen days and submit entirely to him. I easily made an excuse to my parents, and at night I was on my way to the Tyrol.

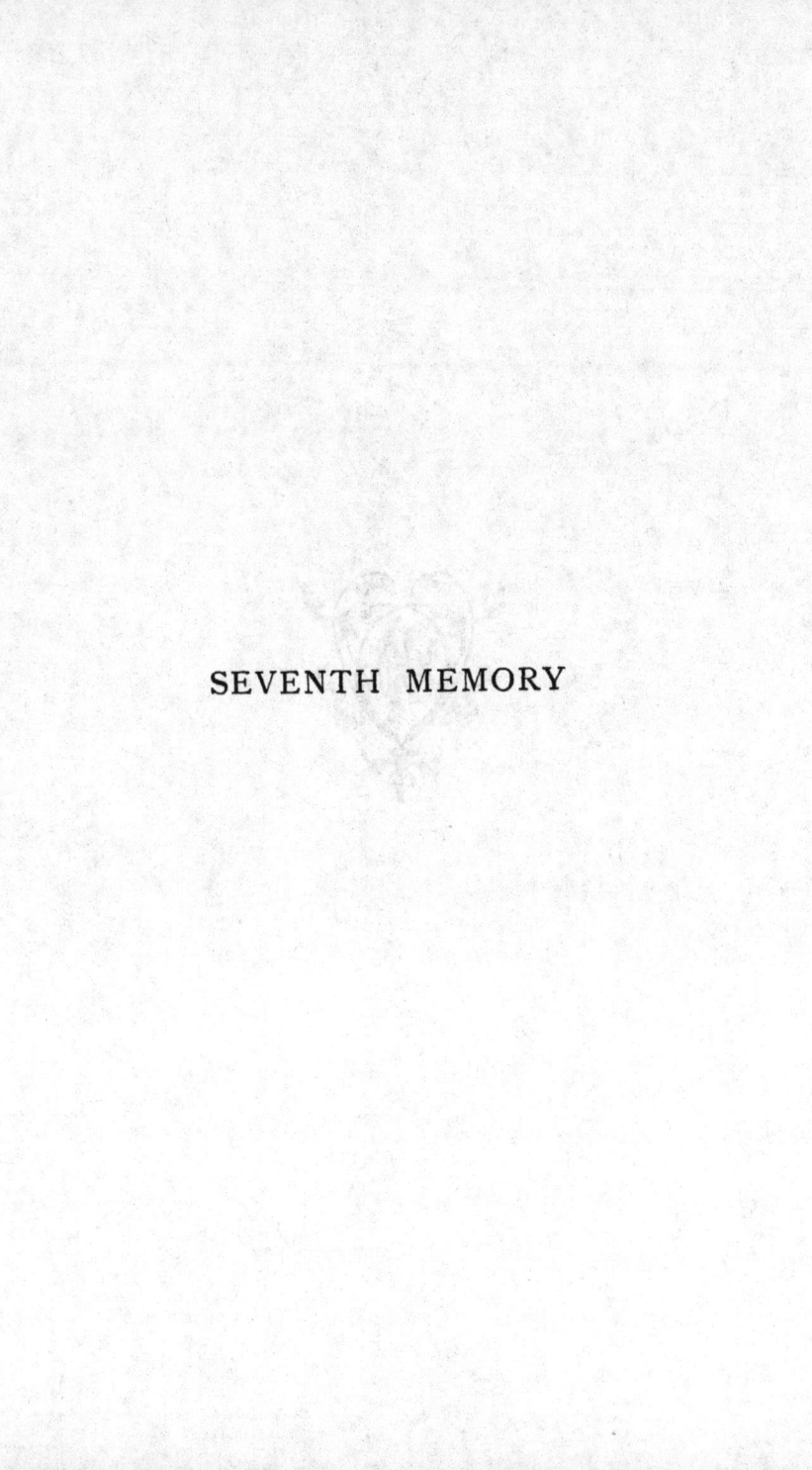

SEVENTH MEMORY

SEVENTH MEMORY.

WANDERING, arm in arm with a friend, through the valleys and over the mountains of the Tyrol, one sips life's fresh air and enjoyment; but to travel the same road solitary and alone with your thoughts is time and trouble lost. Of what interest to me are the green mountains, the dark ravines, the blue lake, and the mighty cataracts? Instead of contemplating them they look at me and wonder among themselves at this solitary being. It smote me to the heart that I had found no one in all the world who loved me more than all others. With such thoughts I awoke every morning, and they haunted me all the day like a song which one cannot drive away. When I entered the inn at night and sat down wearied, and the people in the room watched me, and wondered at the

solitary wanderer, it often urged me out into the
night again, where no one could see I was alone.
At a late hour I would steal back, go quietly up
to my room and throw myself upon my hot bed,
and the song of Schubert's would ring through
my soul until I went to sleep: "Where thou art
not, is happiness." At last the sight of men,
whom I continually met laughing, rejoicing and
exulting in this glorious nature, became so intol-
erable that I slept by day, and pursued my journey from place to place in the clear moonlight
nights. There was at least one emotion which
dispelled and dissipated my thoughts: it was
fear. Let any one attempt to scale mountains
alone all night long in ignorance of the way —
where the eye, unnaturally strained, beholds distant shapes it cannot solve — where the ear, with
morbid acuteness, hears sounds without knowing
whence they come — where the foot suddenly
stumbles, it may be over a root which forces its
way through the rocks, or on a slippery path
which the waterfall has drenched with its spray

— and besides all this, a disconsolate waste in the heart, no memory to cheer us, no hope to which we may cling — let any one attempt this, and he will feel the cold chill of night both outwardly and inwardly. The first fear of the human heart arises from God forsaking us; but life dissipates it, and mankind, created after the image of God, consoles us in our solitariness. When even this consolation and love, however, forsake us, then we feel what it means to be deserted by God and man, and nature with her silent face terrifies rather than consoles us. Even when we firmly plant our feet upon the solid rocks, they seem to tremble like the mists of the sea from which they once slowly emerged. When the eye longs for the light, and the moon rises behind the firs, reflecting their tapering tops against the bright rock opposite, it appears to us like the dead hand of a clock which was once wound up, and will some day cease to strike. There is no retreat for the soul, which feels itself alone and forsaken even among the

stars, or in the heavenly world itself. One
thought brings us a little consolation: the repose,
the regularity, the immensity, and the unavoida-
bleness of nature. Here, where the waterfall
has clothed the gray rocks on either side with
green moss, the eye suddenly recognizes a blue
forget-me-not in the cool shade. It is one of
millions of sisters now blossoming along all the
rivulets and in all the meadows of earth, and
which have blossomed ever since the first morning of creation shed its entire inexhaustible
wealth over the world. Every vein in its leaves,
every stamen in its cup, every fibre of its roots,
is numbered, and no power on earth can make
the number more or less. Still more, when
we strain our weak eyes and, with superhuman
power, cast a more searching glance into the
secrets of nature, when the microscope discloses
to us the silent laboratory of the seed, the bud
and the blossom, do we recognize the infinite,
ever-recurring form in the most minute tissues
and cells, and the eternal unchangeableness of

Nature's plans in the most delicate fibre. Could
we pierce still deeper, the same form-world would
reveal itself, and the vision would lose itself as
in a hall hung with mirrors. Such an infinity as
this lies hidden in this little flower. If we look
up to the sky, we see again the same system —
the moon revolving around the planets, the
planets around suns, and the suns around new
suns, while to the straining eye the distant star-
nebulæ themselves seem to be a new and beautiful world. Reflect then how these majestic
constellations periodically revolve, that the sea-
sons may change, that the seed of this forget-
me-not may shed itself again and again, the
cells open, the leaves shoot out, and the blossoms decorate the carpet of the meadow; and
look upon the lady-bug which rocks itself in the
blue cup of the flower, and whose awakening
into life, whose consciousness of existence, whose
living breath, are a thousand-fold more wonderful than the tissue of the flower, or the dead
mechanism of the heavenly bodies. Consider
8

that thou also belongest to this infinite warp
and woof, and that thou art permitted to com-
fort thyself with the infinite creatures which
revolve and live and disappear with thee. But
if this All, with its smallest and its greatest, with
its wisdom and its power, with the wonders of its
existence, and the existence of its wonders, is the
work of a Being in whose presence thy soul does
not shrink back, before whom thou fallest pros-
trate in a feeling of weakness and nothingness,
and to whom thou risest again in the feeling of
His love and mercy — if thou really feelest that
something dwells in thee more endless and eternal than the cells of the flowers, the spheres of
the planets, and the life of the insect — if thou
recognizest in thyself as in a shadow the reflection of the Eternal which illuminates thee — if
thou feelest in thyself, and under and above
thyself, the omnipresence of the Real, in which
thy seeming becomes being, thy trouble, rest,
thy solitude, universality — then thou knowest
the One to Whom thou criest in the dark night

of life: "Creator and Father, Thy will be done
in Heaven as upon earth, and as on earth so
also in me." Then it grows bright in and about
thee. The daybreak disappears with its cold
mists, and a new warmth streams through shiver-
ing nature. Thou hast found a hand which
never again leaves thee, which holds thee when
the mountains tremble and moons are extinguished. Wherever thou may'st be, thou art with
Him, and He with thee. He is the eternally
near, and His is the world with its flowers and
thorns, His is man with his joys and sorrows.
"The least important thing does not happen
except as God wills it."

With such thoughts I went on my way. At
one time, all was well with me; at another,
troubled; for even when we have found rest and
peace in the lowest depths of the soul, it is still
hard to remain undisturbed in this holy solitude.
Yes, many forget it after they find it and scarcely
know the way which leads back to it.

Weeks had flown, and not a syllable had

reached me from her. "Perhaps she is dead
and lies in quiet rest," was another song forever
on my tongue, and always returning as often as
I drove it from me. It was not impossible, for
the Hofrath had told me she suffered with heart
troubles, and that he expected to find her no
more among the living every morning he visited
her. Could I ever forgive myself if she had left
this world and I had not taken farewell of her,
nor told her at the last moment how I loved her?
Must I not follow until I found her again in
another life, and heard from her that she loved
me and that I was forgiven? How mankind
defers from day to day the best it can do, and
the most beautiful things it can enjoy, without
thinking that every day may be the last one, and
that lost time is lost eternity! Then all the
words of the Hofrath, the last time I saw him,
recurred to me, and I felt that I had only re-
solved to make my sudden journey to show my
strength to him, and that it would have been a
still more difficult task to have confessed my

weakness and remained. It was clear to me that it was my simple duty to return to her immediately and to bear everything which Heaven ordained. But as soon as I had laid the plan for my return journey, I suddenly remembered the words of the Hofrath: "As soon as possible she must go away and be taken into the country." She had herself told me that she spent the most of her time, in summer, at her castle. Perhaps she was there, in my immediate vicinity; in one day I could be with her. Thinking was doing; at daybreak I was off, and at evening I stood at the gate of the castle.

The night was clear and bright. The mountain peaks glistened in the full gold of the sunset and the lower ridges were bathed in a rosy blue. A gray mist rose from the valleys which suddenly glistened when it swept up into the higher regions, and then like a cloud-sea rolled heavenwards. The whole color-play reflected itself in the gently agitated breast of the dark lake from whose shores the mountains seemed to

rise and fall, so that only the tops of the trees
and the peaks of the church steeples and the
rising smoke from the houses defined the limits
which separated the reality of the world from
its reflection. My glance, however, rested upon
only one spot — the old castle — where a presentiment told me I should find her again. No light
could be seen in the windows, no footstep broke
the silence of the night. Had my presentiment
deceived me? I passed slowly through the outer
gateway and up the steps until I stood at the
fore-court of the castle. Here I saw a sentinel
pacing back and forwards, and I hastened to the
soldier to inquire who was in the castle. "The
Countess and her attendants are here," was the
brief reply, and in an instant I stood at the main
portal and had even pulled the bell. Then, for
the first time, my action occurred to me. No
one knew me. I neither could nor dare say who
I was. I had wandered for weeks about the
mountains, and looked like a beggar. What
should I say? For whom should I ask? There

was little time for consideration, however, for the
door opened and a servant in princely livery
stood before me, and regarded me with amaze-
ment.

I asked if the English lady, who I knew
would never forsake the Countess, was in the
castle, and when the servant replied in the affirm-
ative, I begged for paper and ink and wrote her
I was present to inquire after the health of the
Countess.

The servant called an attendant, who took the
letter away. I heard every step in the long halls,
and every moment I waited, my position became
more unendurable. The old family portraits of
the princely house hung upon the walls — knights
in full armor, ladies in antique costume, and in
the center a lady in the white robes of a nun
with a red cross upon her breast. At any other
time I might have looked upon these pictures
and never thought that a human heart once beat
in their breasts. But now it seemed to me I
could suddenly read whole volumes in their feat-

ures, and that all of them said to me: "We also have once lived and suffered." Under these iron armors secrets were once hidden as even now in my own breast. These white robes and the red cross are real proofs that a battle was fought here like that now raging in my own heart. Then I fancied all of them regarded me with pity, and a loftier haughtiness rested on their features as if they would say, Thou dost not belong to us. I was growing uneasy every moment, when suddenly a light step dissipated my dream. The English lady came down the stairs and asked me to step into an apartment. I looked at her closely to see if she suspected my real emotions; but her face was perfectly calm, and without manifesting the slightest expression of curiosity or wonder, she said in measured tones, the Countess was much better to-day and would see me in half an hour.

When I heard these words, I felt like the good swimmer who has ventured far out into the sea, and first thinks of returning when his

arms have begun to grow weary. He cleaves
the waves with haste, scarcely venturing to
cast a glance at the distant shore, feeling
with every stroke that his strength is failing
and that he is making no headway, until at
last, purposeless and cramped, he scarcely has
any realization of his position; then suddenly
his foot touches the firm bottom, and his arm
hugs the first rock on the shore. A fresh reality confronted me, and my sufferings were a
dream. There are but few such moments in
the life of man, and thousands have never
known their rapture. The mother whose child
rests in her arms for the first time, the father
whose only son returns from war covered with
glory, the poet in whom his countrymen exult,
the youth whose warm grasp of the hand is
returned by the beloved being with a still
warmer pressure — they know what it means
when a dream becomes a reality.

At the expiration of the half hour, a servant came and conducted me through a long

suite of rooms, opened a door, and in the fad-
ing light of the evening I saw a white figure,
and above her a high window, which looked
out upon the lake and the shimmering mountains.

"How singularly people meet!" she cried out
in a clear voice, and every word was like a cool
rain-drop on a hot summer's day.

"How singularly people meet, and how singularly they lose each other," said I; and thereupon I seized her hand, and realized that we
were together again.

"But people are to blame if they lose each
other," she continued; and her voice, which
seemed always to accompany her words, like
music, involuntarily modulated into a tenderer
key.

"Yes, that is true," I replied; "but first tell
me, are you well, and can I talk with you?"

"My dear friend," said she, smiling, "you
know I am always sick, and if I say that I feel
well, I do so for the sake of my old Hofrath;

for he is firmly convinced that my entire life
since my first year is due to him and his skill.
Before I left the Court-residence I caused him
much anxiety, for one evening my heart suddenly ceased beating, and I experienced such
distress that I thought it would never beat
again. But that is past, and why should we
recall it? Only one thing troubles me. I have
hitherto believed I should some time close my
eyes in perfect repose, but now I feel that my
sufferings will disturb and embitter my departure from life." Then she placed her hand
upon her heart, and said: "But tell me, where
have you been, and why have I not heard from
you all this time? The old Hofrath has given
me so many reasons for your sudden departure,
that I was finally compelled to tell him I did
not believe him — and at last he gave me the
most incredible of all reasons, and counselled —
what do you suppose?"

"He might seem untruthful," I interrupted,
so that she should not explain the reason, "and

yet, perhaps he was only too truthful. But
this also is past, and why should we recall it?"

"No, no, my friend," said she, "why call it
past? I told the Hofrath, when he gave me the
last reason for your sudden departure, that I
understood neither him nor you. I am a poor
sick, forsaken being, and my earthly existence
is only a slow death. Now if Heaven sends
me a few souls who understand me, or love me,
as the Hofrath calls it, why then should it disturb their joy or mine? I had been reading
my favorite poet, the old Wordsworth, when
the Hofrath made his acknowledgment, and
I said: 'My dear Hofrath, we have so many
thoughts and so few words that we must express many thoughts in every word. Now if
one who does not know us understood that our
young friend loved me, or I him, in such manner as we suppose Romeo loved Juliet and
Juliet Romeo, you would be entirely right in
saying it should not be so. But is it not true
that you love me also, my old Hofrath, and

that I love you, and have loved you for many years? And has it not sometimes occurred to you that I have neither been past remedy nor unhappy on that account? Yes, my dear Hofrath, I will tell you still more—I believe you have an unfortunate love for me, and are jealous of our young friend. Do you not come every morning and inquire how I am, even when you know I am very well? Do you not bring me the finest flowers from your garden? Did you not oblige me to send you my portrait, and—perhaps I ought not to disclose it—did you not come to my room last Sunday and think I was asleep? I was really sleeping—at least I could not stir myself. I saw you sitting at my bedside for a long time, your eyes steadfastly fixed upon me, and I felt your glances playing upon my face like sunbeams. At last your eyes grew weary, and I perceived the great tears falling from them. You held your face in your hands, and loudly sobbed: Marie, Marie! Ah, my dear Hofrath, our young friend

has never done that, and yet you have sent him
away.' As I thus talked with him, half in jest
and half in earnest, as I always speak, I perceived that I had hurt the old man's feelings.
He became perfectly silent, and blushed like
a child. Then I took the volume of Wordsworth's poems which I had been reading, and
said : 'Here is another old man whom I love,
and love with my whole heart, who understands
me, and whom I understand, and yet I have
never seen him, and shall never see him on
earth, since it is so to be. Now I will read
you one of his poems, that you may see how
one can love, and that love is a silent benedic-
tion which the lover lays upon the head of the
beloved, and then goes on his way in raptur-
ous sorrow.' Then I read to him Wordsworth's
'Highland Girl;' and now, my friend, place the
lamp nearer, and read the poem to me, for it
refreshes me every time I hear it. A spirit
breathes through it like the silent, everlasting
evening-red, which stretches its arms in love

and blessing over the pure breast of the snow-
covered mountains."

As her words thus gradually and peacefully
filled my soul, it at last grew still and solemn in
my breast again; the storm was over, and her
image floated like the silvery moonlight upon
the gently rippling waves of my love — this
world-sea which rolls through the hearts of all
men, and which each calls his own while it is
an all-animating pulse-beat of the whole human
race. I would most gladly have kept silent
like Nature as it lay before our view without,
and ever grew stiller and darker: But she
gave me the book, and I read:

> Sweet Highland Girl, a very shower
> Of beauty is thy earthly dower!
> Twice seven consenting years have shed
> Their utmost bounty on thy head:
> And these gray rocks, that household lawn,
> Those trees, a veil just half withdrawn,
> This fall of water that doth make
> A murmur near the silent lake.

This little bay; a quiet road
That holds in shelter thy abode—
In truth, together do ye seem
Like something fashioned in a dream;
Such forms as from their covert peep
When earthly cares are laid asleep!
But, O fair creature! in the light
Of common day, so heavenly bright,
I bless thee, vision as thou art,
I bless thee with a human heart;
God shield thee to thy latest years!
Thee neither know I, nor thy peers;
And yet my eyes are filled with tears.

   With earnest feeling I shall pray
For thee when I am far away:
For never saw I mien or face,
In which more plainly I could trace
Benignity and home-bred sense
Ripening in perfect innocence.
Here scattered, like a random seed,
Remote from men, thou dost not need
The embarrassed look of shy distress,
And maidenly shamefacedness:
Thou wear'st upon thy forehead clear
The freedom of a mountaineer.

A face with gladness overspread!
Soft smiles, by human kindness bred!
And seemliness complete, that sways
Thy courtesies, about thee plays;
With no restraint, but such as springs
From quick and eager visitings
Of thoughts that lie beyond the reach
Of thy few words of English speech:
A bondage sweetly brooked, a strife
That gives thy gestures grace and life!
So have I, not unmoved in mind,
Seen birds of tempest-loving kind—
Thus beating up against the wind.

What hand but would a garland cull
For thee who art so beautiful?
O happy pleasure! here to dwell
Beside thee in some heathy dell;
Adopt your homely ways and dress,
A shepherd, thou a shepherdess:
But I could frame a wish for thee
More like a grave reality:
Thou art to me but as a wave
Of the wild sea; and I would have
Some claim upon thee, if I could,
Though but of common neighborhood.

9

What joy to hear thee, and to see!
Thy elder brother I would be,
Thy father — anything to thee!
   Now thanks to heaven! that of its grace
Hath led me to this lonely place.
Joy have I had; and going hence
I bear away my recompense.
In spots like these it is we prize
Our memory, feel that she hath eyes:
Then why should I be loth to stir?
I feel this place was made for her;
To give new pleasure like the past,
Continued long as life shall last.
Nor am I loth, though pleased at heart,
Sweet Highland Girl, from thee to part;
For I, methinks, till I grow old,
As fair before me shall behold,
As I do now, the cabin small,
The lake, the bay, the waterfall,
And thee, the spirit of them all!

I had finished, and the poem had been to me
like a draught of the fresh spring-water which I
had sipped so often of late as it dropped from
the cup of some large green leaf.

Then I heard her gentle voice, like the first tone of the organ, which wakens us from our dreamy devotion, and she said:

"Thus I desire you to love me, and thus the old Hofrath loves me, and thus in one way or another we should all love and believe in each other. But the world, although I scarcely know it, does not seem to understand this love and faith, and, on this earth, where we could have lived so happily, men have made existence very wretched.

"It must have been otherwise of old, else how could Homer have created the lovely, wholesome, tender picture of Nausikaa? Nausikaa loves Ulysses at the first glance. She says at once to her female friends: 'Oh, that I could call such a man my spouse, and that it were his destiny to remain here.' She was even too modest to appear in public at the same time with him, and she says, in his presence, that if she should bring such a handsome and majestic stranger home, the people would say, she may

have taken him for a husband. How simple
and natural all this is! But when she heard
that he was going home to his wife and children,
no murmur escaped her. She disappears from
our sight, and we feel that she carried the picture of the handsome and majestic stranger a
long time afterward in her breast, with silent and
joyful admiration. Why do not our poets know
this love — this joyful acknowledgment, this calm
abnegation? A later poet would have made a
womanish Werter out of Nausikaa, for the reason
that love with us is nothing more than the prelude to the comedy, or the tragedy, of marriage.
Is it true there is no longer any other love?
Has the fountain of this pure happiness wholly
dried up? Are men only acquainted with the
intoxicating draught, and no longer with the
invigorating well-spring of love?"

At these words the English poet occurred to
me, who also thus complains:

From heaven if this belief be sent,
   If such be nature's holy plan,
Have I not reason to lament
   What man has made of man.

"Yet, how happy the poets are," said she. "Their words call the deepest feelings into existence in thousands of mute souls, and how often their songs have become a confession of the sweetest secrets! Their heart beats in the breasts of the poor and the rich. The happy sing with them, and the sad weep with them. But I cannot feel any poet so completely my own as Wordsworth. I know many of my friends do not like him. They say he is not a poet. But that is exactly why I like him; he avoids all the hackneyed poetical catch-words, all exaggeration, and everything comprehended in Pegasus-flights. He is true — and does not everything lie in this one word? He opens our eyes to the beauty which lies under our feet like the daisy in the meadow. He calls everything by its true name. He never intends to startle, deceive, or

dazzle any one. He seeks no admiration for
himself. He only shows mankind how beautiful
everything is which man's hand has not yet
spoiled or broken. Is not a dew-drop on a
blade of grass more beautiful than a pearl set in
gold? Is not a living spring, which gushes up
before us, we know not whence, more beautiful
than all the fountains of Versailles? Is not his
Highland Girl a lovelier and truer expression of
real beauty than Goethe's Helena, or Byron's
Haidee? And then the plainness of his language, and the purity of his thoughts! Is it not
a pity that we have never had such a poet?
Schiller could have been our Wordsworth, had
he had more faith in himself than in the old
Greeks and Romans. Our Ruckert would come
the nearest to him, had he not also sought consolation and home under Eastern roses, away
from his poor Fatherland. Few poets have the
courage to be just what they are. Wordsworth
had it; and as we gladly listen to great men,
even in those moments when they are not

inspired, but, like other mortals, quietly cherish their thoughts, and patiently wait the moment that will disclose new glimpses into the infinite, so have I also listened gladly to Wordsworth himself, in his poems, which contain nothing more than any one might have said. The greatest poets allow themselves rest. In Homer we often read a hundred verses without a single beauty, and just so in Dante; while Pindar, whom all admire so much, drives me to distraction with his ecstacies. What would I not give to spend one summer on the lakes; visit with Wordsworth all the places to which he has given names; greet all the trees which he has saved from the axe; and only once watch a far-off sunset with him, which he describes as only Turner could have painted."

It was a peculiarity of hers that her voice never dropped at the close of her talk, as with most people; on the contrary, it rose and always ended, as it were, in the broken seventh chord. She always talked up, never down, to people.

The melody of her sentences resembled that of the child when it says: "Can't I, father?" There was something beseeching in her tones, and it was well-nigh impossible to gainsay her.

"Wordsworth," said I, "is a dear poet, and a still dearer man to me, and as one often has a more beautiful, wide-spread, and stirring outlook from a little hill which he ascends without effort, than when he has clambered up Mont Blanc with difficulty and weariness, so it seems to me with Wordsworth's poetry. At first, he often appeared commonplace to me, and I have frequently laid down his poems unable to understand how the best minds of England to-day can cherish such an admiration for him. The conviction has grown upon me that no poet whom his nation, or the intellectual aristocracy of his people, recognize as a poet, should remain unenjoyed by us, whatever his language. Admiration is an art which we must learn. Many Germans say Racine does not please them. The Englishman says, 'I do not understand Goethe.'

The Frenchman says Shakespeare is a boor.
What does all this amount to? Nothing more
than the child who says it likes a waltz better
than a symphony of Beethoven's. The art con-
sists in discovering and understanding what each
nation admires in its great men. He who seeks
beauty will eventually find it, and discover that
the Persians are not entirely deceived in their
Hafiz, nor the Hindoos in their Kalidasa. We
cannot understand a great man all at once. It
takes strength, effort, and perseverance, and it is
singular that what pleases us at first sight seldom
captivates us any length of time.

"And yet," she continued, "there is something common to all great poets, to all true
artists, to all the world's heroes, be they Persian
or Hindoo, heathen or Christian, Roman or German; it is—I hardly know what to call it—it
is the Infinite which seems to lie behind them, a
far away glance into the Eternal, an apotheosis
of the most trifling and transitory things. Goethe,

the grand heathen, knew the sweet peace which
comes from Heaven; and when he sings:

> On every mountain-height
>   Is rest.
> O'er each summit white
>   Thou feelest
> Scarcely a breath.
> The bird songs are still from each bough;
> Only wait, soon shalt thou
>   Rest too, in death.

does not an endless distance, a repose which
earth cannot give, disclose itself to him above
the fir-clad summits?   This background is never
wanting with Wordsworth.   Let the carpers say
what they will, it is nevertheless only the superearthly, be it ever so obscure, which charms and
quiets the human heart.   Who has better understood this earthly beauty than Michel Angelo?
—but he understood it, because it was to him
a reflection of superearthly beauty.   You know
his sonnet:

[La forza d'un bel volto al ciel mi sprona
 (Ch'altro in terra non è che mi diletti),
 E vivo ascendo tra gli spirti eletti;
 Grazia ch'ad uom mortal raro si dona.
Si ben col suo Fattor l'opra consuona,
 Ch'a lui mi levo per divin concetti;
 E quivi informo i pensier tutti e i detti;
 Ardendo, amando per gentil persona.

Onde, se mai da due begli occhi il guardo
 Torcer non so, conosco in lor la luce
 Che mi mostra la via, ch'a Dio mi guide;
 E se nel lume loro acceso io ardo,
 Nel nobil foco mio dolce riluce
 La gioja che nel cielo eterna ride."]

"The might of one fair face sublimes my love,
 For it hath weaned my heart from low desires;
 Nor death I heed nor purgatorial fires.
 Thy beauty, antepast of joys above
 Instructs me in the bliss that saints approve;
 For, Oh! how good, how beautiful must be
 The God that made so good a thing as thee,
 So fair an image of the Heavenly Dove.
 Forgive me if I cannot turn away
 From those sweet eyes that are my earthly heaven,

For they are guiding stars, benignly given
To tempt my footsteps to the upward way;
And if I dwell too fondly in thy sight,
I live and love in God's peculiar light."

She was exhausted and silent, and how could I disturb that silence? When human hearts, after friendly interchange of thoughts feel calmed and quieted, it is as if an angel had flown through the room and we heard the gentle flutter of wings over our heads. As my gaze rested upon her, her lovely form seemed illuminated in the twilight of the summer evening, and her hand, which I held in mine, alone gave me the consciousness of her real presence. Then suddenly a bright refulgence spread over her countenance. She felt it, opened her eyes and looked upon me wonderingly. The wonderful brightness of her eyes, which the half-closed eyelids covered as with a veil, shone like the lightning. I looked around and at last saw that the moon had arisen in full splendor between two peaks opposite the castle, and brightened the lake and the village with its friendly smiles. Never had I seen Nature, never had I seen her dear face so beautiful, never had such holy rest settled down upon my soul. "Marie," said I, "in this resplendent moment, let me, just as I am, confess my whole love. Let us, while we feel so powerfully the nearness of the superearthly, unite our souls in a tie which can never again be broken. Whatever love may be, Marie, I love you and I feel, Marie, you are mine for I am thine."

I knelt before her, but ventured not to look into her eyes. My lips touched her hand and I kissed it. At this she withdrew her hand from me, slowly at first and then quickly and decidedly, and as I looked at her an expression of pain was on her face. She was silent for a time, but at last she raised herself and said with a deep sigh :

"Enough for to-day. You have caused me pain, but it is my fault. Close the window. I feel a cold chill coming over me as if a strange hand were touching me. Stay with me — but no,

you must go. Farewell! Sleep well! Pray that
the peace of God may abide with us. We see
each other again — shall we not? To-morrow
evening I await you."

Oh, where all at once had this heavenly rest
flown? I saw how she suffered, and all that I
could do was to quickly hurry away, summon
the English lady and then go alone in the darkness of night to the village. Long time I wandered back and forth about the lake, long my
gaze strayed to the lighted window where I had
just been. Finally, the last light in the castle
was extinguished. The moon mounted higher
and higher, and every pinnacle and projection
and decoration on the lofty walls grew visible in
the fairy-like illumination. Here was I all alone
in the silent night. It seemed to me my brain
had refused its office, for no thought came to an
end and I only felt I was alone on this earth,
that it contained no soul for me. The earth
was like a coffin, the black sky a funeral pall,
and I scarcely knew whether I was living or had

long been dead. Then I suddenly looked up to
the stars with their blinking eyes, which went
their way so quietly — and it seemed to me that
they were only for the lighting and consolation
of men, and then I thought of two heavenly stars
which had risen in my dark heaven so unex-
pectedly, and a thanksgiving rang through my
breast — a thanksgiving for the love of my angel.

LAST MEMORY

LAST MEMORY.

THE sun was already looking into my window over the mountains when I awoke.
Was it the same sun which looked upon us the
evening before with lingering gaze, like a de-
parting friend, as if it would bless the union
of our souls, and which set like a lost hope?
It shone upon me now, like a child which
bursts into our room with beaming glance to
wish us good morning on a joyful holiday.
And was I the same man who, only a few
hours before, had thrown himself upon his bed,
broken in body and spirit? Immediately I felt
once more the old life-courage and trust in
God and myself, which quickened and animated my soul like the fresh morning breeze.
What would become of man without sleep?
We know not where this nightly messenger

leads us; and when he closes our eyes at night
who can assure us that he will open them
again in the morning — that he will bring us
to ourselves?   It required courage and faith
for the first man to throw himself into the
arms of this unknown friend; and were there
not in our nature a certain helplessness which
forces us to submission, and compels us to
have faith in all things we are to believe, I
doubt whether any man, notwithstanding all his
weariness, could close his eyes of his own free
will and enter into this unknown dream-land.
The very consciousness of our weakness and
our weariness gives us faith in a higher power,
and courage to resign ourselves to the beautiful system of the All, and we feel invigorated
and refreshed when, in waking or in sleeping,
we have loosened, even for a short time only,
the chains which bind our Eternal Self to our
temporal Ego.

What had appeared to me, only yesterday,
dark as an evening cloud flying overhead, be-

came instantly clear. We belonged to one
another, that I felt; be it as brother and sister, father and child, bridegroom and bride, we
must remain together now and forever. It only
concerned us to find the right name for that
which we in our stammering speech call Love.

> " Thy elder brother I would be,
> Thy father — anything to thee."

It was this "anything" for which a name must
be found, for the world now recognizes nothing
as nameless. She had told me herself that she
loved me with that pure all-human love, out
of which springs all other love. Her shudder-
ing, her uneasiness, when I confessed my full
love to her, were still incomprehensible to me,
but it could no longer shatter my faith in our
love. Why should we desire to understand all
that takes place in other human natures, when
there is so much that is incomprehensible in
our own? After all, it is the inconceivable
which generally captivates us, whether in na-

ture, in man, or in our own breasts. Men
whom we understand, whose motives we see
before us like an anatomical preparation, leave
us cold, like the characters in most of our
novels. Nothing spoils our delight in life and
men more than this ethic rationalism which
insists upon clearing up everything, and illu-
minating every mystery of our inner being.
There is in every person a something that is
inseparable — we call it fate, the suggestive
power or character — and he knows neither
himself nor mankind, who believes that he can
analyze the deeds and actions of men without
taking into account this ever-recurring prin-
ciple. Thus I consoled myself on all those
points which had troubled me in the evening;
and at last no streak of cloud obscured the
heaven of the future.

In this frame of mind I stepped out of the
close house into the open air, when a messenger brought a letter for me. It was from
the Countess, as I saw by the beautiful, deli-

cate handwriting. I breathlessly opened it — I
looked for the most blissful tidings man can
expect. But all my hopes were immediately
shattered. The letter contained only a request
not to visit her to-day, as she expected a visit
at the castle from the Court Residence. No
friendly word — no news of her health — only
at the close, a postscript: "The Hofrath will
be here to-morrow and the next day."

Here were two days torn out at once from
the book of life. If they could only be completely obliterated — but no, they hang over me
like the leaden roof of a prison. They must
be lived. I could not give them away as a
charity to king or beggar, who would gladly
have sat two days longer upon his throne, or
on his stone at the church door. I remained
in this abstraction for a long time; but then I
thought of my morning prayer, and how I said
to myself there was no greater unbelief than
despondency — how the smallest and greatest
in life are part of one great divine plan, to

which we must submit, however hard it may be. Like a rider who sees a precipice before him, I drew in the reins. "Be it so, since it must be!" I cried out; "but God's earth is not the place for complaints and lamentations. Is it not a happiness to hold in my hand these lines which she has written? and is not the hope of seeing her again in a short time a greater bliss than I have ever deserved? 'Always keep the head above water,' say all good life-swimmers. As well sink at once as allow the water to run into your eyes and throat." If it is hard for us, amid these little ills of life, to keep God's providence continually in view, and if we hesitate, perhaps rightly, in every struggle, to step out of the common-places of life into the presence of the divine, then life ought to appear, to us at least, an art, if not a duty. What is more disagreeable than the child who behaves ungovernably and grows dejected and angry at every little loss and pain? On the other hand, nothing is more

beautiful than the child in whose tearful eyes
the sunshine of joy and innocence soon beams
again, like the flower, which quivers and trembles in the spring shower, and soon after blossoms and exhales its fragrance, as the sun dries
the tears upon its cheeks.

A good thought speedily occurred to me, that
I could live both these days with her, notwithstanding fate. For a long time I had intended
to write down the dear words she had said, and
the many beautiful thoughts she had confided to
me; and so the days passed away in memory of
the many charming hours spent together, and in
the hope of a still more beautiful future, and I
was by her and with her, and lived in her, and
felt the nearness of her spirit and her love more
than I had ever felt them when I held her hand
in mine.

How dear to me now are these leaves! How
often have I read and re-read them — not that
I had forgotten one word she said, but they were
the witnesses of my happiness, and something

looked out of them upon me like the gaze of a
friend, whose silence speaks more than words.
The memory of a past happiness, the memory
of a past sorrow, the silent meditation upon the
past, when everything disappears that surrounds
and restrains us, when the soul throws itself
down, like a mother upon the green grave-
mound of her child who has slept under it many
long years, when no hope, no desire, disturbs
the silence of peaceful resignation, we may well
call sadness, but there is a rapture in this sadness which only those know who have loved and
suffered much. Ask the mother what she feels
when she ties upon the head of her daughter the
veil *she* once wore as a bride, and thinks of the
husband no longer with her! Ask a man what
he feels when the maiden whom he has loved,
and the world has torn from him, sends him
after death the dried rose which he gave her in
youth! They may both weep, but their tears
are not tears of sorrow, but tears of joy; tears
of sacrifice, with which man consecrates himself

to the Divine, and with faith in God's love and wisdom, looks upon the dearest he has passing away from him.

Still let us go back in memory, back in the living presence of the past. The two days flew so swiftly that I was agitated, as the happiness of seeing her again drew nearer and nearer. As the carriages and horsemen arrived on the first day from the city, I saw that the castle was alive with gaily-dressed visitors. Banners fluttered from the roof, music sounded through the castle-yard. In the evening, the lake swarmed with pleasure-boats. The mœnnerchors sounded over the waves, and I could not but listen, for I fancied she also listened to these songs from the window. Everything was stirring, also, on the second day, and early in the afternoon the guests prepared for departure. Late in the evening I saw the Hofrath's carriage also going back alone to the city. I could not restrain myself any longer. I knew she was alone. I knew she thought of me, and longed for me.

Should I allow one night to pass without at
least pressing her hand, without saying to her
that the separation was over, that the next
morning would waken us to new rapture. I
still saw a light in her window — why should
she be alone? Why should I not, for one
moment at least, feel her sweet presence? Already I stood at the castle; already I was about
to pull the bell — then suddenly I stopped and
said: "No! no weakness! You should be
ashamed to stand before her like a thief in
the night. Early in the morning go to her like
a hero, returning from battle, for whom she is
now weaving the crown of love, which she will
place upon thy head in the morning."

And the morning came — and I was with her,
really with her. Oh, speak not of the spirit as if
it could exist without the body. Complete existence, consciousness, and enjoyment, can only be
where body and soul are one — an embodied
spirit, a spiritualized body. There is no spirit
without body, else it would be a ghost: there is

no body without spirit, else it would be a corpse.
Is the flower in the field without spirit? Does
it not appear in a divine will, in a creative
thought which preserves it, and gives it life and
existence? That is its soul — only it is silent in
the flower, while it manifests itself in man by
words. Real life is, after all, the bodily and
spiritual life; real consciousness is, after all, the
bodily and spiritual consciousness; real being
together is, after all, bodily and spiritually being
together, and the whole world of memory in
which I had lived so happily for two days, disappeared like a shadow, like a nonentity, as I
stood before her, and was really with her. I
could have laid my hands upon her brow, her
eyes, and her cheeks, to know, to unmistakably
know, if it were really she — not only the image
which had hovered before my soul day and
night, but a being who was not mine, and still
could and would be mine; a being in whom I
could believe as in myself; a being far from me
and yet nearer to me than my own self; a being

without whom my life was no life, death was no death; without whom my poor existence would dissolve into infinity like a sigh. I felt, as my thoughts and glances rested upon her, that now, in this very instant, the happiness of my existence was complete — and a shudder crept over me as I thought of death — but it seemed no longer to have any terror for me; for death could not destroy this love; it would only purify, ennoble, and immortalize it.

It was so beautiful to be silent with her. The whole depth of her soul was reflected in her countenance, and as I looked upon her I saw and heard her every thought and emotion. "You make me sad," she seemed on the point of saying, and yet would not. "Are we not together again at last? Be quiet! Complain not! Ask not! Speak not! Be welcome to me! Be not bad to me!" All this looked from her eyes, and still we did not venture to disturb the peace of our happiness with a word.

"Have you received a letter from the Hofrath?" was the first question, and her voice
trembled with each word.

"No," I replied.

She was silent for a time, and then said:
"Perhaps it is better it has happened thus, and
that I can tell you everything myself. My friend,
we see each other to-day for the last time. Let
us part in peace, without complaint and without
anger. I feel that I have done you a great
wrong. I have intruded upon your life without
thinking that even a light breath often withers
a flower. I know so little of the world that I
did not believe a poor suffering being like myself could inspire anything but pity. I welcomed
you in a frank and friendly way because I had
known you so long, because I felt so well in your
presence — why should I not tell all? — because
I loved you. But the world does not understand
or tolerate this love. The Hofrath has opened
my eyes. The whole city is talking about us.
My brother, the Regent, has written to the

Prince, and he requests me never to see you
again. I deeply regret that I have caused you
this sorrow. Tell me you forgive me — and
then let us separate as friends."

Her eyes had filled with tears, and she closed
them that I should not see her weeping.

"Marie," said I, "for me there is but one life
which is with you; but for you there is one will
which is your own. Yes, I confess, I love you
with the whole fire of love, but I feel I am not
worthily yours. You stand far above me in
nobility, sublimity and purity, and I can scarcely
understand the thought of ever calling you my
wife. And, yet, there is no other road on which
we could travel through life together. Marie,
you are wholly free; I ask for no sacrifice. The
world is great, and if you wish it, we shall never
see each other again. But if you love me, if you
feel you are mine, oh, then, let us forget the
world and its cold verdict. In my arms I will
bear you to the altar, and on my knees I will
swear to be yours in life and in death."

"My friend," said she, "we must never wish for the impossible. Had it been God's will that such a tie should unite us in this life, would He, forsooth, have imposed these burdens upon me which make me incapable of being else than a helpless child? Do not forget that what we call Fate, Circumstance, Relations, in life, is in reality only the work of Providence. To resist it is to resist God himself, and were it not so childish one might call it presumptuous. Men wander on earth like the stars in heaven. God has indicated the paths upon which they meet, and if they are to separate, they must. Resistance were useless, otherwise it would destroy the whole system of the world. We cannot understand it, but we can submit to it. I cannot myself understand why my inclination towards you was wrong. No! I cannot, will not call it wrong. But it cannot be, it is not to be. My friend, this is enough — we must submit in humility and faith."

11

Notwithstanding the calmness with which she spoke, I saw how deeply she suffered; and yet I thought it wrong to surrender so quickly in this battle of life. I restrained myself as much as I could, so that no passionate word should increase her trouble, and said:

"If this is the last time we are to meet in this life, let us see clearly to whom we offer this sacrifice. If our love violated any higher law whatsoever, I would, as you say, bow myself in humility. It were a forgetfulness of God to oppose one's self to a higher will. It may seem at times as if men could delude God, as if their small sense had gained some advantage over the Divine wisdom. This is frenzy — and the man who commences this Titanic battle, will be crushed and annihilated. But what opposes our love? Nothing but the talk of the world. I respect the customs of human society. I even respect them when, as in our time, they are over-refined and confused. A sick body needs artificial medicines, and without the barriers, the respect and the prejudices of society, at which we smile, it were impossible to hold mankind together as at present existing, and to accomplish the purpose of our temporal co-existence. We must sacrifice much to these divinities. Like the Athenians, we send every year a heavy boatload of youths and maidens as tribute to this monster which rules the labyrinth of our society. There is no longer a heart that has not broken; there is no longer a man of true feelings who has not been obliged to break the wings of his love before he came into the cage of society for rest. It must be so. It cannot be otherwise. You know not life, but thinking only of my friends, I can tell you many volumes of tragedy.

"One loved a maiden, and the love was returned; but he was poor, she was rich. The fathers and relatives wrangled and sneered, and two hearts were broken. Why? Because the world looked upon it as a misfortune for a woman to wear a dress made of the wool of a shrub in America, and not of the fibres of a worm in China.

"Another loved a maiden, and was loved in return; but he was a Protestant, she was a Catholic. The mothers and the priests bred mischief, and two hearts were broken. Why? On account of a political game of chess which Charles V and Henry VIII played together, three hundred years ago.

"A third loved a maiden, and was loved in return; but he was a noble, she a peasant. The sisters were angry, and quarreled, and two hearts were broken. Why? Because, a hundred years ago, one soldier slew another in battle, who threatened the life of his king. This gave him title and honors, and his great grandson expiated the blood shed at that time, with a disappointed life.

"The statisticians say a heart is broken every hour, and I believe it. But why? In almost every case, because the world does not recognize love between 'strange people,' unless it be

between man and wife. If two maidens love
the same man — the one must fall as a sacrifice. If two men love the same maiden, one
or both must fall as a sacrifice. Why? Cannot one love a maiden, without wishing to
marry her? Cannot one look upon a woman,
without desiring her for his own? You close
your eyes, and I feel I have said too much.
The world has changed the most sacred things
in life into the most common. But, Marie,
enough! Let us talk the language of the world
when we must talk, and act in it, and with it.
But let us preserve a sanctuary where two
hearts can speak the pure language of the
heart, undisturbed by the raging of the world
without. The world itself honors this seclu-
sion, this courageous resistance, which noble
hearts, conscious of their own rectitude, oppose
to the ordinary course of things. The atten-
tions, the amenities, the prejudices of the world
are like a climbing plant. It is pleasant to
see an ivy, with its thousand tendrils and roots,

decorating the solid wall-work; but it should not be allowed too luxuriant growth, else it will penetrate every crevice of the structure, and destroy the cement which welds it together. Be mine, Marie; follow the voice of your heart. The word which now hangs upon your lips decides forever your life and mine — my happiness and yours."

I was silent. The hand I held in mine returned the warm pressure of the heart. A storm raged in her breast, and the blue heaven before me never seemed so beautiful as now, while the storm swept by, cloud upon cloud.

"Why do you love me?" said she, gently, as if she must still delay the moment of decision.

"Why, Marie? Ask the child why it is born; ask the flower why it blossoms; ask the sun why it shines. I love you because I must love you. But if I am compelled to answer further, let this book, lying by you, which you love so much, speak for me:

[„Das beste solte das liebste sin, unb in biser libe
solte nicht angesehen werden nutz unb unnutz, fromen
ober schaden, gewin ober vorlust, ere ober unere, lob
ober unlob ober biser keins, sunder was in ber
warheit das ebelste unb das aller beste ist, bas solt
auch bas allerliebste sin, unb umb nichts anbers ban
allein umb bas, bas es bas ebelst unb bas beste ist.
Hie nach mœcht ein mensche sin leben gerichten von
ussen unb von innen. Von ussen: wan unber ben
creaturen ist eins besser ban bas anber, bar nach
ban bas ewig gut in einem mer ober minner schinet
unb wurket ban in bem andern. In welchem nun
bas ewig gut aller meist schinet, luchtet, wurket unb
bekant unb geliebet wirt, bas ist ouch bas beste unber
ben creaturen; unb in welchem bis minst ist, bas ist
ouch bas aller minst gut. So nu ber mensche bie
creatur hanbelt unb ba mit umb get, unb bisen
unberscheit bekennet, so sol im ie bie beste creatur
bie liebste sin unb sol sich mit flis zu ir halben unb
sich ba mit voreinigen . . .“]

"The best should be the most loved, and in
this love there should be no consideration of
advantage or disadvantage, gain or loss, honor or
dishonor, praise or blame, or anything else, but
of that which in reality is the noblest and best,

which should be the dearest of all; and for no other reason, but because it is the noblest and best. According to this a man should plan his inner and outer life. From without: if among mankind there is one better than another, in proportion as the eternally good shines or works more in one than in another. That being in whom the eternally good shines, works, is known and loved most, is therefore the best among mankind; and in whom this is most, there is also the most good. As now a man has intercourse with a being, and apprehends this distinction, then the best being should be the dearest to him, and he should fervently cling to it, and unite himself with it. . . . . ."

"Because you are the most perfect creature that I know, Marie, therefore I am good to you, therefore you are dear to me, therefore we love each other. Speak the word which lives in you, say that you are mine. Deny not your innermost convictions. God has imposed a life of suffering upon you. He sent me to bear it with you. Your sorrow shall be my sorrow, and we will bear it together, as the ship bears the heavy sails which guide it through the storms of life into the safe haven at last."

She grew more and more silent. A gentle flush played upon her cheeks like the quiet evening gleam. Then she opened her eyes full —the sun gleamed all at once with marvellous lustre.

"I am yours," said she. "God wills it. Take me just as I am; so long as I live I am yours, and may God bring us together again in a more beautiful life, and recompense your love."

We lay heart to heart. My lips closed the lips upon which had just now hung the blessing of my life, with a gentle kiss. Time stood still for us. The world about us disappeared. Then a deep sigh escaped from her breast. "May God forgive me for this rapture," she whispered. "Leave me alone now, I cannot endure more. *Auf wiedersehen!* my friend, my loved one, my savior."

These were the last words I ever heard from her. But no — I had reached home and was lying upon my bed in troubled dreams. It was past midnight when the Hofrath entered my room. "Our angel is in Heaven," said he; "here is the last greeting she sends you." With these words he gave me a letter. It enclosed the ring which she had given me, and I once had given her, with the words: "*As God wills.*" It was wrapped in an old paper, whereon she had some time written the words I spoke to her when a child: "What is thine, is mine. Thy Marie."

Hours long, we sat together without speaking. It was a spiritual swoon which Heaven sends us when the load of pain becomes greater than we can bear. At last the old man arose, took my hand and said: "We see each other to-day for the last time, for you must leave here, and my days are numbered. There is but one thing I must say to you — a secret which I have carried all my life, and confessed to no one. I have

always longed to confess it to some one. Listen
to me. The spirit which has left us was a beautiful spirit, a majestic, pure soul, a deep, true
heart. I knew one spirit as beautiful as hers —
still more beautiful. It was her mother. I loved
her mother, and she loved me. We were both
poor, and I struggled with life to obtain an hon-
orable position both on her account and my own.
The young Prince saw my bride and loved her.
He was my Prince; he loved her ardently. He
was ready to make any sacrifice and to elevate
her, the poor orphan, to the rank of Princess.
I loved her so that I sacrificed the happiness of
my love for her. I forsook my native land and
wrote her I would release her from her vow. I
never saw her again, except on her death-bed.
She died in giving birth to her first daughter.
Now you know why I loved your Marie, and
prolonged her life from day to day. She was
the only being that linked my heart to this life.
Bear life as I have borne it. Lose not a day in
useless lamentation. Help mankind whenever

you can. Love them and thank God that you
have seen and known and loved on this earth
such a human heart as hers—and that you have
lost it."

"*As God will,*" said I, and we parted for life.

———

And days and weeks and months and years
have flown. Home is a stranger to me, and a
foreign land is my home. But her love remains
with me, and as a tear drops into the ocean, so
has her love dropped into the living ocean of
humanity and pervades and embraces millions—
millions of the "strange people" whom I have
so loved from childhood.

———

Only on quiet summer days like this, when
one in the green woods has nature alone at heart,
and knows not whether there are human beings
without, or he is living entirely alone in the
world, then there is a stir in the graveyard of
memory, the dead thoughts rise again, the full
omnipotence of love returns to the heart and

streams out from that beautiful being who once looked upon me with her deep unfathomable eyes. Then it seems as if the love for the millions were lost in the love for the one, my good angel, and my thoughts are dumb in the presence of the incomprehensible enigma of endless and everlasting love.

www.ingramcontent.com/pod-product-compliance
Lightning Source LLC
Chambersburg PA
CBHW011406010726
47495CB00009B/2796